To Protect His Brother's Baby

Linda Goodnight

LOVE INSPIRED

INSPIRATIONAL ROMANCE

LOVE INSPIRED®

INSPIRATIONAL ROMANCE

Recycling programs for this product may not exist in your area.

ISBN-13: 978-1-335-59830-1

To Protect His Brother's Baby

Love Inspired
22 Adelaide St. West, 41st Floor
Toronto, Ontario M5H 4E3, Canada
www.LoveInspired.com

Printed in U.S.A.

He looked up at her from beneath his hat brim.

"You asked me about a housekeeping job."

"Yes." Her pulse sped up.

"You've taken good care of the place. Improved it, even."

Was he going to let her stay? "I tried."

"You did. Even though I'm not much on goats or chickens."

"I'll have to sell them anyway when I leave, and I'll take down the pens so they're not a bother."

"They're not. What I mean is—" he swallowed "—you're in a bad spot."

Thanks, Cowboy Obvious. "I can take care of myself."

"Understood. You've made that clear. But that baby you're carrying is my niece or nephew."

She hadn't considered that, but he was right. Half-right anyway. "I suppose so."

"No *suppose* to it. I have an obligation."

The tension jumped back on her shoulders and clamped down harder than a vise.

"No. You do not."

She didn't want to be an obligation to anyone. That was part of the reason she didn't go home to her family…

Linda Goodnight, a *New York Times* bestselling author and winner of a RITA® Award in Inspirational Fiction, has appeared on the Christian bestseller list. Her novels have been translated into more than a dozen languages. Active in orphan ministry, Linda enjoys writing fiction that carries a message of hope in a sometimes-dark world. She and her husband live in Oklahoma. Visit her website, lindagoodnight.com, for more information.

Books by Linda Goodnight

Love Inspired

Sundown Valley

To Protect His Children
Keeping Them Safe
The Cowboy's Journey Home
Her Secret Son
To Protect His Brother's Baby

The Buchanons

Cowboy Under the Mistletoe
The Christmas Family
Lone Star Dad
Lone Star Bachelor

Love Inspired Trade

Claiming Her Legacy

Visit the Author Profile page at LoveInspired.com for more titles.

Thou wilt shew me the path of life: in thy presence in fulness of joy; at thy right hand there are pleasures for evermore.

—*Psalm* 16:11

For my youngest daughter,
who inspired the story. And for the glory
of Messiah Jesus, my Savior and King.
Thank You for giving me the peace that passes
understanding even through the storms of life.

Chapter One

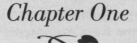

She wasn't driving too fast. At least, she didn't think she was, though Taylor Matheson's mind had been somewhere else as it tended to be too frequently. Especially lately.

But suddenly, in a lightning bolt of awareness, she spotted a chicken.

In the road.

Right in the middle of the curvy, graveled road.

There was really nothing Taylor could do, but, being a tender heart, she slammed on her brakes anyway. Wrong move. The car skidded, fishtailed. A collision of bird and Toyota was inevitable.

The car slid to a stop. Dust flew. In her rearview mirror Taylor saw the little hen. Still in the middle of the country road, though she no longer happily pecked at gravel.

Feeling like ten kinds of awful, Taylor hopped out of the vehicle, hurried to the poor little hen and picked her up. As if the hen knew she'd met the guilty party, she pecked Taylor's hand.

It hurt, but Taylor figured she had it coming.

"I won't be mad if you won't," she said to the bird. "Poor baby. I'm sorry. Really, I am."

As gently as possible, Taylor carried the wounded

hen to the car, all the while eyeing the small, ramshackle farmhouse a hundred yards off the road.

"Did you come from over there?"

Of course she had. There was no other place nearby. Unfortunately.

Taylor was not too keen on encountering the old woman who lived alone in that run-down house, was rumored to hate people and could shoot your eye out at twenty paces. Flora Grimley.

The dozen or so no-trespassing signs posted for a good quarter-mile swath of the leaning, rusted, overgrown fence accented the woman's dislike of human beings.

In the few months Taylor had lived in this tiny rural community of Mercy, Oklahoma, a town dangerously close to her family in Sundown Valley, she had thankfully managed to avoid her nearest neighbor. And her family.

Taylor did not like conflict. She'd rather leave than fight, and often did, which worked well for a travel blogger. Except her traveling days were over for a while. Which meant her livelihood was over. Unless she could think of some other job to do for the next few months...or years.

But Taylor refused to worry. Things had a way of working out. Take the ranch where she now lived. Her husband or boyfriend or ex-whatever-he-was may have been a faithless jerk, but he'd left her with a ranch. Sort of. Another thing she wouldn't worry about.

She was actually having fun turning the house into a thriving little property.

The chicken squawked. Taylor stared down at her. This part was not fun.

About the time she decided to drive off and take the bird with her, the old woman appeared on the porch, toting the rumored shotgun that looked like a cannon to Taylor, and bellowed, "What are you doing out there? Trying to rob me?"

"No, ma'am," Taylor yelled back. "Is this your chicken?"

"Did you kill one of my hens?"

"She's not dead."

Flora waved a bony arm. "Bring her up here and let me see."

All this was said in the rudest, gruffest tone Taylor had heard since being terrified by the Wicked Witch of the West when she was seven. Flora Grimley looked scrawny, but was reportedly as tough as wet leather. And mean as a badger.

With dread in her chest but determined to do right by the hen who couldn't help belonging to a mean woman, Taylor drove the rutted, weedy lane to the house and got out with the chicken.

"Her leg is hurt. Broken, I think."

Flora grunted. "Put her on the porch. I'll wring her neck and fry her up."

"No!" Taylor drew the hen closer to her chest. The hen pecked her hand again. "She looks okay except for her leg."

"What else am I to do with a one-legged chicken? She's good for nothing now."

"Shouldn't we try to fix her?"

"Fix her? Why, that's the silliest thing I ever heard of. The only way to fix a one-legged chicken is in the skillet."

"I could try. I'm pretty good with animals." Being raised in the country, she'd learned a lot. Although her sister Harlow had never let her *do* anything, she had watched and learned.

"Huh. Ridiculous." The old lady stood, shotgun at her side, baggy dress loose and faded, with an expression Taylor thought might be consideration. "All right, then—take her. She's worthless to me."

"When she gets well, I'll bring her back."

"No, you won't. She'll never lay another egg. She's worthless. Take her."

"Yes, ma'am. Thank you, ma'am."

Flora Grimley's faded gray eyes narrowed. "What's your name, girl? I don't know you. What are you doing messing around out here on my road?"

"Taylor Matheson. I'm your neighbor. I live on the farm about a mile that way." She tried to motion with her thumb but didn't want to disturb the now-calmed chicken.

"You the gal living in that roaming cowboy's place?"

"Yes, ma'am. I'm his wife…er…widow."

"Widow?" For a second, Taylor thought she spotted a flicker of sympathy. Just as quick, the faded eyes sharpened. "I'm not a bit surprised he's dead. Good-for-nothing cowboy always sneaking around doing things he ought not to."

That was Cale, all right. A good-for-nothing sneak. He'd fooled her, lied to her and humiliated her in the worst possible way.

The ache in Taylor's throat expanded until she could say nothing in return.

"Men," Flora barked. "They should all be shot. Especially men like him, spouting his Jesus-talk, which in my books is about as bad you can get. Using religion to manipulate people. Liars, hypocrites, the lot of them. No good for nothing."

Although she'd never heard Cale mention Jesus except to take His name in vain, Taylor had to take exception to the woman's generalization. "My grandpa is a fine Christian man. He practices what he preaches."

"Then, he's as rare as teeth on that hen. Or he's got you boondoggled. Probably that. You look the type." Flora's bony finger motioned toward Taylor's car. "Go on. If you're going to whine about her and make me out the villain, take that worthless chicken and go."

"If she lays eggs again, I'll bring them to you."

"No use lying. Now, get off my property."

Flora Grimley whirled around, stomped inside the house and slammed the door.

Still shaking, but feeling relieved that the hen

had been spared the death penalty, Taylor drove the rest of the way to the ranch house she now called home. It was the only thing she'd gotten out of her short-lived marriage that turned out not to be a marriage at all.

"What a fool I was." *Fool, fool, fool.*

Her belly gyrated, a reminder that the ranch house wasn't the only thing she'd gotten from Cale.

"I won't regret you." She patted the rapidly expanding mound. "But I do regret your daddy. Flora Grimley is right about him."

When the people of tiny Mercy, Oklahoma, population 232, had learned she was a widow and pregnant, they had welcomed Taylor like a lost daughter and helped her get started at the ranch. Most of them anyway. In five months, she'd turned the abandoned ranch into a little farm. Again thanks to the locals' generosity and advice.

Raised on a ranch, she knew how to plant seeds and care for animals, although her sisters had done most of the work. They considered her inept, useless, the baby sister who needed mothering after her terrible injuries in the car crash that killed their parents.

Taking the hen into the kitchen, Taylor placed her on the countertop to begin her exam.

She didn't like thinking about the car wreck, but the memory pushed in on her at odd times. She'd moved all over America and still the tragedy followed her. She'd been in that car. Her sisters hadn't.

They didn't know what really happened that rainy night.

Taylor had only been eight when the accident occurred, but she'd never told another person, especially not her sisters.

Sometimes holding the truth inside hurt so much that she couldn't catch her breath. To combat the feeling, each time the memory raised its ugly head she headed off on her next travel adventure. Nothing like a new place and a blog deadline to take her mind off things better forgotten.

"Don't think about it. Focus." With gentle hands, she explored the hen's body, which was mostly feathers, and found no injury other than the broken leg.

"And to think Flora wanted to fry you. Poor thing." She stroked the red head. "I can fix you. I watched Harlow and Monroe—they're my big sisters—patch up animals all my life." And she could learn about anything from the internet.

In minutes she'd splinted and wrapped the hen's lower leg and carried her out to the chicken pen to a wire crate.

"You'll be with your friends, Esther, but they can't hurt you if you're inside this cage. Okay?" She'd decided on Esther because the biblical queen had survived some tough times, just like the hen.

Promising to check on her later, Taylor unloaded the car and set to work in the kitchen. With the travel blog floundering due to inactivity, she needed another form of income. Milly and Walt at the Mercy Mercantile had given her an idea.

Taylor was full of ideas. That was part of her wanderlust. It also got her in a lot of trouble.

But that didn't matter. She landed on her feet, even when those feet were swollen and no longer able to climb rocks or hike thirty miles in the heat.

She'd find a way. She always did. She'd make a life for her and baby, and someday, when her courage was strong and she'd proven herself to be something more than a flaky, gullible, inept kid, she'd drive her baby eighteen miles to meet the rest of the Matheson family. Until then, phone calls would have to do.

When anyone asked about the baby's daddy, she'd play the sad widow and hope no one ever discovered what she'd done.

Wilder Littlefield blinked his eyes against the fatigue pulling at him like lead hands. As his truck lights swept the two-lane highway, he leaned over the steering wheel and squinted into the growing dusk.

"Want me to drive the rest of the way?" This from Pate Allbrook, Wilder's fellow rodeo cowboy and usual traveling buddy. Sharing expenses made the paychecks stretch further. Sharing the wheel let each of them catnap the many miles between rodeos.

"We're nearly to the cutoff to my place, but I'm

too beat to go farther than that. You can take my truck on to your house."

Pate lived in Sundown Valley, the next town over. Wilder figured he might be able to stay awake long enough to drive the eighteen miles and back, but he was powerfully tired.

"What about your trailer?" Toted along behind the big diesel pickup was a combination living quarters and horse trailer bearing the steady horse that helped Wilder win. Without Huck, he was just a guy who could throw a rope.

"Won't take long to unhook first. Then take my truck. Go home, get some shut-eye, see your woman and then bring it back. I won't need a vehicle for at least three days. I'm planning to sleep that long."

Pate chuckled. "I hear that."

Wilder rotated his neck and shoulders as they drove through the tiny whistle-stop of Mercy, past the still-open Mercantile, a shuttered post office and a few houses lit from within. Although a number of citizens ran businesses out of their homes, the town proper rounded out with a senior citizen center, a water office that also housed the town council, two churches, a gas station–bait shop next to the Mercantile, a sometimes-open burger joint and a surprisingly large school.

In two minutes flat, he left the town behind and aimed the truck down a gravel road past Miss Grimley's place. The old woman stood in almost darkness on her porch, broom in hand.

As his lights swept over her, Wilder tapped his horn in greeting. She glared at his truck and shook her fist.

"Friendly sort, isn't she?" Pate asked.

"The Lord's working on her. She almost waved."

Pate grinned. "Always the evangelist."

Wilder took some teasing for his deep faith, although the teasing was gentle. Cowboys respected a man with strong beliefs. Many of them shared his faith.

Cowboys. He'd never wanted to be anything else, and for the first time since he'd hit the pro rodeo circuit at eighteen, Wilder was on track to make the National Finals this year. A few more rodeos, a few more wins. Only the top fifteen ropers would make it, and he aimed to be one of them.

He was past thirty years old. Time was no longer on his side. Neither was his bruised and battered body. With his prime quickly fading, it was this year or never. He knew it with a deep-down, uneasy certainty.

He was scared to even think about what he'd do if he didn't make it. He had plans, a dream for the future, all of which rested on a big payout this year.

Rounding the final curve, his ranch house came into sight.

"Home, sweet home," he murmured.

Man, he was tired. Though he only returned to his Three Nails Ranch a few times a year, usually when a rodeo brought him close enough, tonight the small country cottage looked as good as a mansion. Someday, he'd be able to come home and stay forever. He sure looked forward to that day.

Pate shifted in the passenger seat. "Say, Wilder, is someone staying at your place?"

"No. Of course not." Never. He'd let a friend house-sit once only to return to the biggest mess he'd ever seen. His house had become party central, complete with trash, old food and empty cans and bottles. He'd needed a week to clean it all up again. Since then, no one stayed at his place.

"Then why are the lights on?"

Wilder blinked, squinted, blinked again. Was he in the right place?

His house, which he'd left locked and empty, looked different. The broken gate he'd never gotten around to fixing now hung straight and was painted a bright blue. There were pots of sunny yellow flowers on either side of a blue front door. And a goat roamed the front yard.

Wilder Littlefield did not own a goat.

Sure enough. Someone was in his house.

"Take my truck and go on home," he said to Pate.

"Not on your life, pal. I'm not leaving until you check this out. There's a woman in there, I'm pretty sure."

"Why do you say that?"

"Flowers on the porch. A blue gate *and* door. Frilly curtains in the windows. Come on. Would you have done that?"

"No."

"Me neither. Could be one of your girlfriends come home to roost."

"You know better."

"You might be strait-laced, but you're still a man and the ladies like you."

"Not that much." Nobody, not one woman he'd ever dated, and there weren't that many, had ever come close to making him feel domestic.

The idea that he might accidentally fall in love and consider marriage scared him mindless. So he never dated a woman more than twice. Hard-and-fast rule. Marriage, kids and whatever came with them were not in his future. Too risky. He would not become like the stranger who'd fathered him.

Horses, yes. Wife and kids, no.

"I'll unhook the trailers and put Huck away while you have a look." Pate grinned as if he thought the matter amusing. "Holler if you need help."

"Go home. I'll have whoever this is packed up and out of here in ten minutes. Then, I'm sleeping until Sunday."

He considered calling the county sheriff but changed his mind. Anyone who painted blue doors and planted flowers was no threat to a man who handled 500-pound steers for a living.

Slinging his duffel over one shoulder, Wilder marched up to the front door and stuck the key in the lock.

Someone had some explaining to do.

* * *

Taylor happily banged pots and pans in the tidy yellow kitchen. She'd painted the walls herself and sewn the ruffled print curtains for the window over the sink. A touch of robin's egg blue to the pantry door matched the front door and gate. The place had been so lifeless when she'd arrived, but now it was bright and cheerful.

Though Cale had made her miserable, his sweet little house made her happy. She worried about the failing travel blog but tried to look on the bright side. She had a home. Granted, the home wasn't exactly in her name. *Yet.* She'd figure that part out later.

Cale had specifically told her that no one knew about this ranch but him. She hadn't questioned it at the time, so besotted was she with the handsome, confident bull rider, but after his death she understood. He hadn't told his *wife.* This ranch was his hideaway for his mistresses. Plural. And she was one of them, although she hadn't known.

"Don't think about that." She bounced her palms against her temples. "Block, block, block." She was adept at blocking. She'd drowned out her sisters' voices for years.

Busy behind the kitchen island with her latest project, she turned the music up on her phone to drown out negative thoughts. With earbuds in, she didn't hear the door open, didn't know another soul was anywhere on the property until movement in the doorway between kitchen and living room caught her attention.

She looked up. And gasped. The spoon in her hand clattered to the floor.

"Who are you? Get out of my house."

A cowboy of considerable size, with shoulders as wide as a door, stared at her from very brown eyes. He wasn't particularly handsome, not like Cale, but he had a boatload of rugged masculine appeal. Even the bump on a nose that had obviously been broken at some point added to his manliness.

In faded jeans, scuffed boots and a white T-shirt, he looked relaxed but weary, a duffel bag slung over one shoulder. As if he had a right to invade her home.

She was alone, far from the nearest neighbor— Flora Grimley—who probably wouldn't help her anyway.

"*Your* house, you say? Since when?" The cowboy had a ragged, husky kind of voice that made the hair on Taylor's arms tingle.

"Since my husband died and left it to me." Sort of. Cale had *told* her about the ranch. He hadn't exactly handed over the deed. And Cale wasn't exactly her husband.

Those, however, were unnecessary details. The point was, this ranch *should* have been hers because she was carrying Cale's baby, who was technically Cale's only heir that she knew of. So this big, muscled, not-so-scary cowboy needed to go away.

He dropped the duffel bag onto the tile and leaned a shoulder against the doorframe. Actually, he sagged against it as though he needed something to hold him up. "Your husband?"

Was the guy a parrot?

"Yes."

Suddenly, another cowboy, this one smaller and wiry, again with noticeable shoulders, appeared behind cowboy number one.

Two strange men.

Taylor tensed. She reached for the cast-iron skillet still sitting on the stove. "Get out."

"No can do."

"She's pretty." This from cowboy number two, whose eyes danced with merriment as though he found the situation hilarious. Which it was *not*. "Looks dangerous. You gonna wrestle her down like a steer?"

The comment so incensed Taylor that she wielded the skillet higher and started around the island toward them. Her arm wavered. Cast iron was heavy.

With the island no longer between them, her body was now in full view. Both men dropped their gazes to her belly. Their expressions registered surprise.

Cowboy number two clapped a hand on the first man's shoulder. "Wilder, Wilder, what have you done?"

The man called Wilder spun on his boot toward the other cowboy. "Pate, you know better. Go home. Shelby will be worrying about you. I don't know who this woman is or what she's doing here, but I'll sort this out."

Pate lifted both hands. "All right. I see you got some fences to mend or some such, so I'll give you some privacy."

"This isn't what it looks like."

"No?" Pate laughed softly. "If you say so."

Wilder growled, "Get!"

"I'm getting, I'm getting."

Pate, staring at Taylor as if she was some sort of alien, backed his way out of the room, still chuckling.

When the front door snapped shut, cowboy Wilder took a step closer.

Taylor moved behind the island again to put some space between them, although the cowboy looked capable of ripping the island out of the way if he so wished.

She hoped he didn't want to.

But what *did* he want?

"Ma'am," Wilder said in that husky drawl that tickled her ears and a spot behind her rib cage. "I'm not sure what's going on here, but I don't know you from Adam. You're saying this is your ranch and your husband left it to you?"

Taylor's back ached from standing over the counter all afternoon, but she was not ready to release her heavy weapon. "Yes. He did. So, I guess you must have been his friend, right? I suppose if you were wanting to bunk here for the night, you can stay in the barn and then be on your way in the morning."

Knowing Cale as she now did, he probably didn't have many *decent* friends. She'd make sure to lock the doors and brace them with a chair, like they did on TV. She didn't know if that worked or not, but she'd feel better doing it.

The cowboy shook his head and emitted a soft chuckle.

"No, ma'am. I won't stay in the barn. I'm staying in my bedroom, where I always sleep."

"You will not."

"Yes. I will." His tone was calm and quiet but made of steel.

"You won't. I'll call the sheriff."

"Call him. He's an old friend."

She blinked. "He is?"

"Yes, ma'am. Go ahead. Call him."

When he put it that way, the last person she wanted involved was the sheriff. He'd evict her, maybe arrest her for impersonating a widow. Laurel Maxwell would print the police report in the county newspaper just like she had for years. Taylor's family in Sundown Valley would find out and her dreams of returning home as a successful woman who could stand on her own two feet would die a humiliating death.

Before she could think up an adequate reply,

Wilder—a cool name for a cowboy, she thought—planted both boots in front of her, looked her in the eyes and said, "I don't know what loony train you're riding on, lady, or what scam you're running, but I'm Wilder Littlefield. I don't have a wife. Never had one. Don't *ever* want one. This property is mine. *I* am not your husband, but I *am* the owner of Three Nails Ranch."

Taylor's whole body began to tremble. This guy was lying. He had to be.

But why would he say such a thing if it wasn't true?

And if he wasn't lying, she was in real trouble.

Chapter Two

The woman's eyes widened. She took a step back and then another. She still wielded the black cast-iron skillet but Wilder saw her trembling arm and started worrying about her.

He didn't like that he cared, but he was made that way. Anyone weaker or hurt or upset worried him. This woman appeared to be all three. Plus, pregnant.

Whew. That was a load of worry to carry around in his saddlebags.

"Better put that down before you hurt yourself."

The wobbly arm stiffened. She was gutsy. He'd give her that. He would not, however, give her his house or his bed.

"I'm not going to hurt you," he said. "Put it down."

"That's what all killers say right before they pull out a massive knife and start slashing."

Wilder sighed. He was way too tired for this.

"Lady, you're shaking. You're going to collapse. If you fall and hit this hard floor, you'll hurt yourself and that baby. Then, I'll feel terrible and have to call an ambulance and answer a lot of questions when all I really want is a good long nap."

As if a reminder of the baby was all it took, the

woman heaved the skillet onto the island. *His* island. And rubbed her biceps as if they hurt.

He stared at her through blurry eyes, taking stock of her and whatever had happened in his house in the five months or so since he'd last been here.

Except for the round belly, she was a petite woman. Dark hair was scraped up into a messy bun on top of her head. Her delicate, heart-shaped face was almost childlike, but there was sorrow in her blue eyes. He guessed her to be in her late twenties.

Blue eyes, dark hair and an innocent face, a nice combination on a woman. His own mother had looked that way once, from the photos she'd shown him, but eventually the sorrow and hard times had left their mark.

He'd inherited his mother's thick brown hair but he'd gotten brown eyes from his worthless male parent, whom he hadn't learned about until he was sixteen. Since that painful revelation, every time he looked in the mirror he was reminded of the parent who'd never been there, the one who'd rejected both Wilder and his mother.

Resentment rose up in him like a virus.

He figured he had more praying to do to forgive the man.

Rolling his stiff shoulders, Wilder rubbed a hand over the back of his neck and tried to make sense of what was going on. His brain was too tired to figure this out, but from the looks of his property, the pretty, pregnant, spunky woman had been here a while.

She hadn't said anything, so he prodded. "Let's start with the basics. What's your name? Why are you squatting in my house?"

"Taylor Matheson. I am *not* a squatter. My baby inherited this property."

The lie upset him. "Are you telling people that I'm the father of your child? We both know that's not true."

"Of course not." She looked appropriately offended. "I don't even know you."

"I sure don't know you. Show me your deed."

Her mouth dropped open. She made a small, distressed noise. Her eyes darted to one side.

Awareness settled over Wilder. Pretty, innocent-looking Taylor Matheson was conning him. "Obviously, you don't have a deed."

"Not yet. But this *is* my baby's property. My late husband told me so."

"So this is your house, plus you're a widow too. Pregnant with a late husband's baby. That's rather convenient, don't you think? Most con artists come up with a better story."

Taylor's pretty little feathers ruffled up. He was making her mad. Well, too bad. Normally, he'd have pity on a pregnant, clearly misguided woman who needed help, but he was so tired he was about to lie down on the shiny tile floor.

Shiny. His floor had never looked this good before. Clean as a whistle and polished to a gleam.

He sure hadn't left it that way.

At least she hadn't damaged the place.

"I'm neither a squatter nor a con artist. If you'll just let me explain—"

"Lady," he started, not wanting to hear any more lies.

"I'm Taylor," she insisted.

"Taylor, after a long rodeo and a longer day, I've just driven sixteen hours straight to get home, pulling a horse trailer. My head is too fuzzy to make sense of you. So, please, pack up your belongings and go back to wherever you came from."

"I will not. Not until you prove me wrong."

With a loud groan, Wilder dropped his head back and stared at the ceiling. Clean. Freshly painted. Not a cobweb to be seen.

"Clearly, we have a misunderstanding. Your husband, if you really are a widow, gave you the wrong address. If you'll let me get some shut-eye, I'll help you figure out where you belong tomorrow. Or whenever I wake up. Maybe Sunday."

"It's only Tuesday."

"I know. Do you have family you can call?"

"No." She blinked those blue eyes enough times for him to know something more was coming. "Well, yes, but no."

"Yes, you have family. No, you can't call them. Why not?"

Taylor gnawed her bottom lip, her face a study in distress. "I just can't."

Okay. He got that. Sometimes family, as he well knew, was no family at all.

There he went again, feeling sorry for her. If she was a con artist, she was good enough to play on his sympathies. And man, did he have a truckload of those, especially for a damsel in distress.

A man who ignored a woman in need wasn't a man at all. He'd learned that from his mother and had spent his childhood trying to be grown-up enough to help her. To his great regret, a boy was not a man. Sometimes an adult male was not much of a man either, but that was a different story.

Was Taylor Matheson really needy or was she in some kind of trouble? Maybe she was running from the law or an abusive husband who didn't want the baby.

He understood about that as well. Another reason he was soft on women, especially pregnant ones.

"This husband of yours. What's his name?"

"Late husband. He died at a rodeo six months ago."

She didn't seem too broken up about it. "Rodeo? Who was he? Maybe I knew him."

"Cale Gadsden."

Wilder blinked, rubbed a hand over his face and blinked again. Had she said who he thought she'd said? Or was his exhausted mind playing some really dirty tricks on him?

"Cale Gadsden, the pro bull rider?"

"Yes."

He squinted, trying to make sense of this stunning new information. "Cale's dead?"

"Yes. Did you know him?"

"Not well." But well enough to know he now had no choice except to help Taylor Matheson however he could. "I didn't know he died."

Wilder pinched the bridge of his nose. Shouldn't he be sad about a man's death? Especially Cale's? Shouldn't she, his supposed widow, seem more upset? Not to mention a few other women, including Cale's wife, who Wilder was reasonably certain was not the pregnant woman standing before him.

Sin was ugly and Cale Gadsden majored in it.

Thoughts whirling, heart troubled and confused, Wilder hoisted his duffel bag.

"I can't handle any more tonight. We'll figure something out in the morning."

"Where are you going?"

He sighed, his shoulders sagging. "My camper. It's parked in the driveway."

Where Wilder doubted he'd sleep a wink.

Taylor waited until the wide-shouldered cowboy exited the house before rushing to the front door to click the dead bolt. If he really owned this house, he had a key and could get in whether she locked the door or not. If he wasn't the owner, the lock meant she was safe.

But what if he, not Cale, *was* the real owner?

Wilder was lying. He had to be.

Had Cale told him about the ranch too, and he actually knew Cale had died so he decided to take over?

Twitching the window curtain to one side, Taylor watched the cowboy in the porch light. Duffel bag over his shoulder, moving as if exhausted, Wilder Littlefield headed to a long horse trailer parked in the driveway. Although she'd never been inside one, she recognized the type with space for the cowboy in front and the horses in back. He opened the door, glanced back in her direction and stood in the light from inside the camper for a long moment before ducking his head and stepping inside.

A niggle of guilt pecked at Taylor's conscience the way the little hen, Esther, had pecked at her hand. If this really was his ranch, he was a nice man to take the camper while she remained in his house.

Considerate. Kind. Respectful.

The light in the camper snuffed out.

The cowboy wasn't lying about his fatigue.

Had he been telling the truth about the rest? Had Cale lied to her even about owning this ranch that had become a sanctuary for her and the baby?

Worrying her bottom lip, Taylor returned to the island and her project.

She loved it here. Even though money was tight, she felt successful, fulfilled, useful. She'd made friends in Mercy.

What if Wilder forced her to leave? Where would she go now?

Would she be forced to call her sisters and Poppy and admit the mess she'd made of her life, face the humiliation and crawl on hands and knees back to Matheson Ranch? A failure. Someone who couldn't run her own life, much less that of a tiny baby.

Taylor studied the supplies she'd gathered to start her own cottage industry. That's what Milly at the Mercantile called it. After seeing the improvements Taylor had made at the ranch, Milly and Walt had encouraged her to use her homesteading skills— Walt's words—to create wholesome, clean, natural products people would buy. Such things were popular these days. Taylor often chose them for herself.

So here she was about to make soap for the first time ever.

Thankfully, she hadn't started the scary part of the process when the rugged cowboy burst in on her.

Donning her safety goggles and gloves, she snapped a few photos for her blog before slowly mixing the ingredients.

She found the process interesting and hoped her blog readers would, as well. Making soap didn't exactly qualify as travel but if she spun the article properly, she could convince followers and sponsors that a cottage industry was a great place to travel. Which wasn't completely true but had enough truth to be convincing. Anything to keep the affiliate checks coming in.

Add the very popular idea that every ingredient she used was natural, even the lye, since it came from wood ash, and she'd pull in more millennials. Her peers were all about natural, plant-based whatever. She just wanted them to keep reading.

As she slowly stirred the lye flakes into the partially frozen goat milk, the trouble with Wilder Littlefield overrode thoughts of her blog.

He said he'd known Cale, yet he hadn't heard about Cale's death. Such news usually traveled fast, but perhaps Cale's family had requested privacy and covered up the truth. Or rather truths. Lots of them. They certainly wouldn't want his many indiscretions made public.

Cale's death had released an entire Pandora's box of information Taylor had not known. She'd been lied to. Her bull-riding cowboy had never loved her. He'd used her. Nor was she the only woman in Cale's life as he'd claimed. Not even close. He saw other women when on the road, and worst of all, he had a legal wife who was not Taylor.

She'd married a bigamist whose fast life had caught up with him at the end.

What would Wilder think when he learned that Cale had died at a rodeo, but not during a bull ride and not because of an angry bull?

Chapter Three

Wilder opened one eye. He hoped it was Sunday, but his body refused to believe he'd slept that long.

Light streamed in the tiny window at the top of the trailer door. In his exhaustion, he'd forgotten to pull the curtain.

Stumbling from the narrow bunk that barely provided room for a man his size, he tried to remember what town he was in. Was he entered in a rodeo tonight?

He gazed out the window. Sunlight reflected off a blue front door.

Blue.

As memory of the previous night rushed in, Wilder jerked upright, bumped his head and came fully awake.

His ranch. The pregnant woman. Some nutty business about her husband.

Cale.

He sat back down on the edge of the bunk and put his face in his hands.

Cale was dead. And he hadn't known. No reason for him to have been informed and yet, he hurt a little that no one had told him.

Swallowing his pride and reluctance, he prayed

for Cale's family and sincerely hoped Cale had made peace with the Lord before his death. The man was the worst stereotype of hard-living, partying, womanizing rodeo cowboys.

Womanizing.

His thoughts zipped to the sweet-faced woman inside his house. Was she really Cale's widow? Or one of his mistresses?

He tried to remember what Cale's wife looked like, but he had only met her once. He was pretty sure she was blonde. And tall. Which Taylor was not.

He didn't want to feel sorry for her, but if she'd been hoodwinked by Cale and left alone, pregnant and believing she owned a ranch, she deserved his sympathy.

He still wanted his house back, though. He wanted a hot shower, clean clothes and a good breakfast. All of which waited for him inside his own home.

They had to talk.

Still in the same clothes he'd worn yesterday, he tugged on his boots and left the camper to approach the front door of the house.

He reached for the doorknob, but then dropped his hand to his side and stared at the blue door.

There was a strange woman inside. Would he be rude to walk in without a warning? Should he knock first? Open the door and call out?

How did a man enter his own home when a woman he didn't know occupied it?

What time was it anyway? Would she be up yet? He'd heard pregnant women needed lots of sleep. He didn't want to disturb her.

"Don't be ridiculous," he muttered. "She's the interloper, not you."

He didn't want to barge in and scare her. Or worse, embarrass them both. He was a modest man, after all, a Christian who didn't roam around in his underwear.

He sure didn't want to think about Taylor in hers.

As Pate had reminded him last night, Wilder was devout in his faith, but he was still very much a man. He admired women, but he also respected them, thanks to a mother who'd have thumped his head if he didn't and to Jesus who expected no less.

So here he remained on his own front porch, trying to figure out the most respectful way to get into his own house.

A nanny goat rounded the corner of the porch and watched him with a curious tilt to her head.

"I don't know where you came from," he told her, "but I live here. Maybe not often, but I still own the place, and I've never been much for goats."

She baaed at him. Sort of the way Taylor had done. Baa-baa, go away.

Wilder wasn't going anywhere except inside this house.

He raised his fist to knock and then, irritated by the entire situation, dug in his pocket for the key.

As he started to insert the key into the lock, the front door opened.

Barefoot, but thankfully dressed in khaki shorts and a baggy T-shirt covering the baby bump, Taylor stood in the entry. Fatigue reddened her blue eyes. She, apparently, had not slept as well as he had.

Naturally, he felt bad for her. It was his fault she couldn't rest. He'd barged in last night and upset her.

"Good morning." Her tone, as bright and sunny as the yellow flowers at his feet, did not match her eyes.

Faker.

"'Morning. We need to talk."

"Yes, we do." She stepped to one side and let him in. This time she didn't wield a skillet. She'd either decided he was no threat or had come to the conclusion that a skillet was no match for a man of his size.

"Poppy always said serious talk goes easier on a full belly," she said. "I hope you like pancakes."

"Who doesn't?"

"I'm not a great cook but my pancakes aren't bad. How many can you eat?"

"A dozen maybe, depends on the size."

Taylor blinked a couple of times as she considered the capacity of any man to eat that much.

What could he say? He was a big man with a big

appetite who worked hard and hadn't eaten since sometime yesterday.

"I'll make more batter," she said finally.

"Got any eggs?"

She blinked again in a way he was starting to find both amusing and charming. "Plenty. The girls are laying like champs."

"The girls?"

"My hens."

"Hens." He now owned chickens. And a goat. What was this world coming to? He was a cowboy, not a farmer.

"How many do you want?"

"Hens? Or eggs?"

A flicker of a smile teased her pretty mouth. Inwardly, Wilder groaned. He hadn't wanted to notice her in any way, especially her bow mouth with the defined M and full lower lip.

So why had he made a joke and made her smile?

"Eggs. At least four. But I'll cook them myself. After a shower." He stood awkwardly for a moment, trying to figure out how to navigate this bizarre situation before finally saying, "Excuse me."

From the living room, Wilder turned left toward the hall and the guest bathroom. No way was he going right toward the larger bedroom and bath— *his* bed and bath—until he knew for sure where she'd set up camp.

Chickens. Goats. Flowers. Frilly curtains.

Wilder shook his head at all the changes.

Including the addition of a woman.

He was pretty sure he'd entered the twilight zone.

Taylor went back into the kitchen. She'd been up since six when the overzealous rooster hit a high note, caring for him and the animals while keeping an eye on the camper trailer. All the while, she'd wondered about Wilder Littlefield and what this new dawn would bring.

She'd heard him step up on the porch and, when he didn't come in, had wondered if he even had a key. Which would mean he did not own the house, and that gave her hope.

Except when she'd first arrived at the ranch months ago, she'd taken the key from under the doormat, a silly place to hide a key. Everyone looked there first.

Maybe he'd expected it to still be there.

Then she'd seen the flash of silver in his hand and her hopes of getting rid of him tumbled. Not wanting to rile him in case he really was the ranch's owner, which she feared he was, Taylor had opened the door and let him in.

This morning, Wilder didn't seem quite as formidable.

He didn't smile, but he didn't demand she pack up and leave the premises either.

To further appease the cowboy, she'd stirred up batter for pancakes using fresh eggs and goat milk.

The way to a man's heart, after all, was through his stomach. Poppy used to say that all the time.

The milk tasted a little different but a goat was cheaper to buy than a cow and basically fed herself, all while producing milk for cheese and soap and yogurt. And she mowed the lawn.

Win-win-win.

Taylor hoped the cowboy didn't notice the different taste.

Smiling a little to think of anyone consuming nearly a dozen pancakes and four eggs, she set out more flour, eggs and milk.

The man was big but fit, his belly as flat as the pancakes she was making. Not an inch of fat on him.

Lately, everything she ate made her fatter.

Taylor placed her hand on her belly.

What if she had twins growing in there? The thought scared her silly. She was nervous enough about having one baby to care for. How would she travel for work and care for twins?

"Where's my shaving equipment?"

Taylor jumped at the intrusion of a man's gravelly voice. She spun toward the doorway leading out of the kitchen and into the living room.

Wilder stepped into the small eat-in kitchen. The room felt even smaller with him inside. "Didn't mean to startle you."

Although the unshaven whiskers gave him a rakish appearance, he looked fresher now, more awake, his brown eyes soft as they lit on her. Fully dressed right down to his boots, his hair, though neatly combed, was still damp and curling around his earlobes.

Looking at him gave her a funny feeling.

"I wasn't expecting you."

"Obviously."

"What I mean is, I boxed up anything that pertained to Cale for donation." She hadn't wanted the reminders. Besides, she'd been so angry and hurt, she'd have burned them if her practical side hadn't reminded her that someone could get some use out of his things. Milly said she should have a garage sale and make some money, so she was entertaining the idea of that as well.

"I wondered why my clothes were in boxes in the laundry room."

"I haven't gotten around to driving them to Centerville." Or setting up that garage sale.

"I'm grateful for that." The corner of his mouth lifted. "A man needs his clothes."

"Right." She fidgeted, off-balance, uncomfortable, anxious. She was starting to believe he owned the ranch, which put her in a terrible position. "The pancakes are in the warmer. How do you want your eggs?"

"I can cook them."

Taylor bristled. "So can I."

In fact, she'd fight for the right to cook, just as she fought to make her own way in life. The one thing she wanted to make clear to everyone: Taylor Elizabeth Matheson did not need a caregiver.

"Touchy," he muttered.

An awkward silence fell on the kitchen while he rummaged in the refrigerator for the butter and jelly, and she fried the eggs. Tension tightened her shoulders.

Wilder poured himself a glass of milk and sipped. Watching out of the corner of one eye, Taylor held her breath.

His face screwed up. "What is this?"

"Goat milk."

"Oh." He set the glass aside and took another from the cabinet, filling it with water.

Though he didn't complain, he clearly wasn't a goat milk fan. Well, too bad. She hadn't exactly been expecting company, except for a friend who planned to come by later to show her how to set eggs under one of the hens that gave every indication of wanting to hatch babies.

She glanced toward the cowboy, now leaning his back against the center island, sipping the glass of water, his eyes roaming over every change she'd made to the kitchen.

He hadn't criticized but she wondered what he thought.

He looked strong as a bull, and she had the thought that he might be a bull rider like Cale. If so, why hadn't he known about Cale's death?

So many questions she needed to ask, and Wilder

likely had more. Lots more. She dreaded the coming conversation.

While the prospect of baby chickens got her excited, maybe she should text Cindy not to come today. Or ever, depending on what happened in the next hour.

When the eggs were ready, the cowboy accepted them with a polite "thank you" and carried his overflowing plate to the small, square table in the corner of the kitchen.

Taylor poured herself a glass of juice and anxiously pulled out a chair opposite him.

He glanced up. "Aren't you eating?"

"I ate earlier." Not much. She'd been too jittery about this coming confrontation.

He didn't look angry or mean, but a person never knew.

He reached a hand toward her. She stared at the wide palm, uncomprehending, until he said, "Let's pray."

If that wasn't the weirdest thing a man near her age had ever said to her, she didn't know what was.

Wilder had already closed his eyes and bowed his head, so she bowed hers too, but watched him from beneath her lashes.

Feelings fluttered in the pit of her stomach as she saw his thick, black lashes brush the tops of his cheeks and watched his mouth, surrounded by dark whiskers, move.

He asked God to bless the food and then briefly prayed for guidance to "resolve this mess."

Though she hadn't prayed in years and didn't claim to be a Christian, Taylor couldn't help but echo the cowboy's amen.

This was a mess all right, but she'd caused it and didn't expect help from God, whom she'd ignored since she was eight years old.

Except to compliment the food, which she thought was stretching the truth, Wilder ate in silence. When he finished, he carried his dishes to the sink and put away the condiments.

Surprised by his courtesy, Taylor remained seated, watching him, wondering about this man who'd invaded her space and now held her future in his big, powerful hands.

When he settled into his chair again and looked at her with an unreadable expression, Taylor's nerves jumped under her skin. Her breath shortened, and the baby protested with a couple of backflips.

"Start at the beginning," he said.

"Which one?"

He gave a short laugh. "Start with Cale."

"Oh." She wasn't about to tell him how romantic her bull-riding cowboy had been. Nor would she admit that Cale had swept her off her feet, but that she'd insisted on marriage before she'd slept with him. That was her private business.

It was also her private business that Cale had

never legally married her. The liar. As long as she could play the widow, the better her chances of remaining in this house.

"When did you marry him?"

"October 17 of last year." It was now May.

She'd thought Cale's idea of a whirlwind wedding after only a three-week courtship, just the two of them in Las Vegas, was romantic. Little had she known that he was literally sneaking off so no one would know. He'd told his wife he had a rodeo event, a hurtful fact Paige Gadsden had thrown in her face when they'd both shown up at Cale's funeral.

She wasn't admitting any of that either. If this was Cale's ranch, she wasn't leaving, even if she didn't have a marriage license. And if it wasn't his ranch, she was in a world of hurt.

"When did he die?" He asked the question as if the words were sharp and cut him.

"November." She closed her eyes for a second to get her composure. As angry and hurt as she was, she couldn't forget the horror of watching Cale die. "Twenty-first."

She'd spent Thanksgiving holed up in a hotel alone, grieving and trying to sort out the wreckage of her life. The next day she'd stiffened her spine, packed her bags and taken a post-Thanksgiving ski trip for her travel blog, unaware that she was carrying a child.

"I'm sorry."

So was she. Sorry she'd married the man or thought she had. Sorry for the pain she'd caused his wife and family. Sorry for all the lies Cale had told that brought her to this season of abject humiliation.

Wilder's wide hand slid across the table, turned her palm upright and placed his on hers. His skin was rough, hard, but his eyes were soft.

"Taylor," he said, his husky voice gentle, "you seem like a nice person, but Cale tricked you."

He knew.

Taylor swallowed. And lied through her teeth. "I don't know what you mean."

Wilder breathed in through his nose and looked up at the ceiling as if imploring God for help.

"I'm sorry to be the one to break the news, Taylor. I really am. I didn't know about Cale's death—we travel in different associations—but I know this. You're not married to Cale Gadsden. You couldn't have been."

Tears sprang to her eyes. She batted them, fighting against showing weakness.

He wasn't telling her anything she hadn't already learned, but hearing the words from his mouth brought the shock and shame roaring back in full force. She'd escaped the gossip by moving to this quiet rural area far from Colorado, but now Wilder knew what a fool she'd been.

Jerking her hand from his, she slashed at her

eyes and glared at him. Her cheeks burned. "How could you possibly know that?"

With a weary sigh, he gazed at her for a long moment with what could only be sympathy.

The oven clock ticked. The refrigerator rumbled on. And from outside, the rooster crowed. Later she'd recall it crowed three times. A biblical sign of great betrayal.

When at last he spoke, Wilder's quiet voice was tinged with sadness.

"Because Cale Gadsden, the man you thought you married, was my brother."

Chapter Four

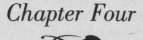

Wilder watched helplessly as the pretty, pregnant non-widow battled her emotions. She needed to cry but she fought like a tiger not to. He'd feel a lot better if she'd let out all the rage and heartache she was bound to feel, although he had to admit a crying woman wrecked him.

Instead, she jerked her chin a tad higher, cheeks red as the ketchup he'd eaten on his eggs, and said, "So, if what you say is true, then you share—" she stopped and rephrased "—you must have shared this ranch with Cale. Brothers in partnership. Right?"

She looked so hopeful, he hated to tell her the truth. If he had Cale here right now, he'd wring the man's neck. God forgive him for thinking ill of the dead, but the evidence of Cale's reputation for misusing women was sitting right here in front of him. From what Wilder could tell, Taylor was a nice person and even if she wasn't, no one deserved to be lied to and mistreated in such an ugly manner.

"I'm sorry. No."

She blinked a half dozen times and swallowed, her throat convulsing as she fought back tears.

"No partnership?"

Gaze holding hers, his sympathy meter off the scale, Wilder shook his head. "No."

If he wasn't careful, he'd get up out of this chair, pull her into his arms and comfort her. Silly notion, given they were perfect strangers, but it was that messed-up sympathy meter of his. The thing gave him fits sometimes. Today was one of the worst ever.

He'd never encountered a situation quite like this. And he sure hoped he never did again.

Taylor's hands twisted together against the tabletop.

Fragile. Vulnerable. Suffering.

The too-descriptive words marched through his mind like a cadet band in a Fourth of July parade.

Awkward silence hung between them, throbbing with questions and a dilemma bigger than both of them.

Finally, when he could bear it no longer, Wilder stopped the writhing fingers with a squeeze.

Wide blue eyes flashed up at him.

He probably shouldn't have touched her. They didn't know each other. But the feel of her small, soft hands beneath his, cold as ice, made him feel as if they did, as if he was somehow the answer to her problems.

His responsibility meter was every bit as sensitive as his sympathy scale.

He was definitely not responsible for Taylor, her baby or the situation she was in. Or for the fact that she'd taken up residence in his home.

But his blood kin was.

He gave the small fingers two quick pats and pulled his hands away. "Hey, it'll be okay."

She gave a short, mirthless laugh. "How?"

He said the only thing that made any sense to him at the moment. His default. His go-to. "Do you believe in prayer?"

God had carried him through tougher things than this.

"Not much."

"I do. God has a way of working things out even when they seem impossible to us. We need to pray for direction."

We. Again, as if any of this was his problem.

She sidestepped his comment. That bothered him a little. He didn't understand people who rejected Jesus. Didn't they realize that life was easier, more peaceful, when a man could toss his problems on Jesus's shoulders and expect things to get better?

"If you're really Cale's brother—" Taylor drew her hands into her lap where he was pretty sure she was twisting her fingers into noodles again "—why didn't you know about his death? Why didn't you attend the funeral?"

Wilder sighed. That thorny bush again. "As you mentioned last night, not every family is close. I barely knew him."

Fact was, they'd met only a few times in his life, just enough for Wilder to know that Cale and their father were cut from the same cloth.

When he was sixteen, after his mother died, he'd had high hopes of being embraced by his biological family. The meeting turned out to be a painful kick in the teeth from both father and son. Stray dogs don't belong with the pedigreed.

"How could you not know your own brother?"

"Half brother. Different moms. I didn't grow up with my biological father." He normally didn't share that information with anyone, but given the circumstances, Taylor deserved an answer.

"Oh. I'm sorry."

So was he. "I doubt if Cale ever mentioned me. Did he?"

"No. We were only together a short time before he died. I never even met his parents until the funeral." Her pretty bow mouth pulled down at the corners. "Now I know why."

Anger toward his half brother bubbled up again. Of course Cale hadn't introduced her to family. She was a mistress, not a wife, a toy he would have soon tossed aside and forgotten if he hadn't died. Taylor would have ended up like Wilder's mother. Alone with a baby whose father had moved on to a less burdensome woman.

"But he told you about my ranch."

"He claimed it was his and that he'd bought it just for us. A getaway, a place we'd retire to someday." Tears welled up in her eyes. She bit down on her back teeth and hissed like a riled snake.

She was getting angry. Good. Anger, he could deal with. Tears, not so much.

"I believed him," she said with enough vehemence to tense the veins in her neck. "I believed everything he told me. That's why I'm here. I really thought the ranch was his property, and that my baby had a right to be here."

"He shouldn't have treated you this way, Taylor. It was wrong. You have every right to be furious." And hurt. Judging by the grief and betrayal in her eyes, she was still more wounded than angry.

Who could blame her? She was in a bad spot. Real bad.

He wondered how Cale had known about the Three Nails Ranch. Their few conversations had mostly been Cale warning him to stay away from his family, because Wilder's presence upset Cale's mother.

All Wilder could say in response was, "What about *my* mother?"

Cale's reply had earned the bull rider a sore jaw and later an apology. Wilder was not a man given to violence, but nobody spoke ill of the woman who'd birthed him and raised him alone when not doing so would have made her life easier.

"I was a fool, so in love with who I thought Cale was that I lost my good sense. We moved way too fast. I should have waited."

"Hey, we all do crazy things for love."

Not that he'd know, but he'd heard other guys say it.

She offered him a watery smile. "Thank you for that. Being jilted and publicly humiliated is hard. Telling someone else about it is equally as embarrassing."

He was feeling so sorry for her he was afraid of doing something really stupid.

"It's okay. Your secret is safe with me." He wasn't exactly a blabbermouth, and to be honest, the last thing he wanted to do was explain why a pregnant woman had been living in his house for what appeared to be several months.

But he figured he'd have to tell folks something.

In a tiny burg like Mercy, everyone knew everyone else and he had no doubt there had been talk.

As he ruminated this new, unexpected concern, Taylor interrupted him with another.

"I don't suppose you could use a live-in housekeeper for a few months, could you? Unpaid, of course."

The question jolted him. A live-in housekeeper? The urge to do something foolish grew stronger. A dozen nonsensical ideas flashed through his head. He threw every one of them on the ground, tied them with a piggin' string and walked away just as he did from a roped calf.

"I'm barely ever here, Taylor. I don't need a housekeeper."

"I understand." She pushed back from the table.

"Well, I'll figure something out. Will you give me a few days?"

What could he say? "Sure. Of course."

His trailer wasn't *that* uncomfortable.

He stood too, awkward again. "Save the coffee. I'll want more after I look after Huck."

She nodded but turned away, and he was certain she was once more hiding tears.

Cale's fault. Except Cale wasn't here to face the consequences. Wilder was. Wilder, who'd been born with the responsibility gene his half brother lacked.

Like it or not, that baby was blood kin, Wilder's nephew, a little kid like he'd once been who'd had no say in his parentage.

So Wilder figured he had to do something. He just didn't know what it would be.

After the front door snapped shut with a quiet snick, and boot thuds disappeared from the porch, Taylor let herself cry for five minutes. Then she washed her face, powdered her nose and finished the blog she'd started yesterday.

When Wilder didn't return and she'd posted the blog with a few photos, she carried the first aid kit she'd found in Wilder's bathroom out to the chicken pen. Wilder's bathroom, not hers, not Cale's.

The tears tried to start up again but she set her teeth like granite and focused on the animals. None of this was their problem.

The May morning, though sunny, was cool, and the air sweet and clean with early summer blooms. Dew sparkled on the grass, dampening Taylor's toes above her flip-flops.

Inside the chicken-wire enclosure, Esther, the hen, seemed reasonably content in her crate, her splint and bandage intact, so Taylor gathered the other hens' eggs into a basket. Recalling Wilder's penchant for a lot of food, she was happy to get so many.

The girls, as she thought of them, clucked around the small pen pecking at bugs, bits of grass, and food scraps and crushed eggshells she'd saved for them. According to Jordy Fitts, hens needed the extra calcium to keep their shells strong.

Strong, healthy chickens were happy chickens. She wanted happy animals on her little farm.

As she put the last warm egg into the basket and stepped out into the sunshine to water her garden, reality sank in. This was not her farm. She had to leave.

She wouldn't be here to see her tomatoes or snow peas ripen or to taste the sweet juiciness of her very first cantaloupe.

A boulder of heaviness settled on her chest.

What would she do with her chickens? And the goat?

Wilder, apparently, wasn't here often enough to want them. There hadn't been a living creature on the place when she'd arrived. The ranch was usually empty. Cale had told the truth about that, at least. She'd have to sell them.

But who would care for Esther? Not Flora Grimley, for sure.

Taylor leaned her back against the door of the chicken house, fighting despair. Again. Hormones were getting the best of her today.

To her left, she spotted movement. Wilder, the cowboy with mountains for shoulders, exited the barn leading a large buckskin horse. This must be the "Huck" he'd mentioned.

The animal playfully snuffled the back of Wilder's neck. The cowboy scrunched those massive shoulders and chuckled as he opened a gate leading into a long, open lot. The laugh, warm and husky, carried across the expanse of green grass to Taylor's ears.

Wilder Littlefield was a nice guy, she decided, though an enigma. She was still shocked that he and Cale were half brothers. Brothers who didn't know each other well enough to be contacted when one of them died. That was weird.

As hard she tried to keep her sisters at arm's length, she'd want to know if something happened to one of them. Fact was, they talked by phone at least once a week. Harlow sent her photos and videos of her and her husband Nash's son, Davis. Monroe kept up a running dialogue about special-needs dogs and the new love of her life, Nathan Garrison, who had restored the old Persimmon Hill Guest Ranch.

Even though they were physically separated, the way she liked it, they remained emotionally close.

She loved her family. She just didn't want them to run her life.

Wilder and Cale, on the other hand, didn't even like each other. Now, that was sad.

Other than both being rodeo cowboys, they were very different. Or seemed to be so far.

Wilder didn't notice her watching as he swung into the saddle and trotted the buckskin down the long arena lot next to the barn. When he began swinging a rope over his head, she couldn't resist going closer.

She climbed up on the first rung of the metal fence, belly bumping against the middle rail, to watch. There was something especially manly about a working cowboy and his horse. Both strong and fit, muscles rippling in tandem.

Wilder swirled the rope overhead, nice and easy, as if there was nothing hard about it. She knew better. Both her sisters were cowgirls. Monroe had been a barrel racer in high school, but neither was good with a rope. Taylor had tried a few times too, only to end up laughing, encased in a tangled trap of her own making.

When Wilder let the loop fly, easily catching the horns of a roping dummy, Taylor wondered if he was a calf roper by trade. If so, that explained why he and Cale hadn't encountered each other often. Cale had traveled with the PBR, an organization for bull riders only. He sneered at regular rodeo as somehow inferior.

Wilder roped the dummy a few more times, slow and easy, putting little stress on the horse. She didn't know a lot about rodeo, especially roping, but she knew a good horse was crucial to success in any timed event and cowboys treated their mounts especially well.

As he turned the horse and started back down the arena, he spotted her and lifted a hand.

Feeling oddly pleased, Taylor waved in return.

He rode up to the fence railing.

Taylor pushed a lock of windblown hair out of her face. "This must be Huck."

"Best horse in the business."

"Are you a calf roper?"

"Tie-down. Yep." He patted the side of the horse's neck. "Usually, I let him rest after an event, but he wanted to stretch this morning."

"He told you that?"

Wilder grinned. "Yep. After he spent most of sixteen hours yesterday in the back of a trailer, I don't blame him." His grin faded, expression growing serious. "A person can do a lot of thinking on a horse's back."

"Is that what you were doing? Thinking?"

"And praying."

"About your brother?"

"About you. But yes, Cale too." He dismounted. Instead of filling her in on this heavy thinking of his, he asked, "What are you going to do with all those eggs?"

He'd been thinking about her. Was he looking for a way to gracefully get rid of her?

She wanted to ask but didn't. She'd inadvertently put the man in a bad spot.

"I'll sell some to Milly and Walt at the Mercantile, and save the rest for you, I guess."

"Those you cooked this morning were real good. Fresh always are."

"That's what Milly says. Customers are willing to pay more for fresh."

Considering the heaviness of the situation hovering over them like a black cloud, a conversation about fresh eggs seemed out of place. But the money would come in handy when she left here.

He wanted her to leave but she didn't want to. At least not until after the baby arrived. She'd built her proverbial nest on this little ranch-turned-farm.

How much time would he give her before he booted her to the curb?

Reins in hand, Wilder began leading Huck toward the barn. Without giving the action any real thought, Taylor kept pace with man and horse by walking along the rail fence that separated them.

"He's a beautiful horse."

"You know horses?"

"Some. I grew up on a little ranch. We always had horses."

"I thought you weren't close with your family."

She hadn't said that. "Our relationship is complicated."

Pausing in the shadow leading inside the barn, he looked at her for a long moment. "I understand."

He didn't. He couldn't.

She let the topic slide away as she followed him into the barn. She'd been inside here many times since December when she'd escaped an uncomfortable family dinner. Aware she was pregnant and still reeling from the unexpected news herself, she'd been unwilling to share that information with anyone. Certainly not her sisters, who would have swept her up in a whirlwind and taken over her life.

Soon after, she'd moved into what she thought was Cale's ranch.

"I made a few changes in here. Nothing drastic." She had been too busy with the garden and her animals.

"I noticed." Pausing in the alleyway, Wilder unbuckled the girth and began unsaddling the big buckskin. "My tack looks in great shape. Thanks."

She'd cleaned the leather, polished the iron and reorganized the tack room, determined to keep everything in good repair for the future day when she'd buy a horse and teach her child to ride.

The effort seemed foolish now. Her child would never use this barn or equipment.

"Why so many saddles with only one horse?"

"Practice tack. A friend in the next town over raises roping calves. He pastures my practice horses."

"You don't practice on Huck?"

He rubbed his hands over the animal's damp back. "Huck's too important to practice on much. I save him for competition."

"That's interesting. I'd think he needs practice too."

"I generally give him a short, easy tune-up before an event, and he's good to go. If he was younger, greener, he'd get more work."

After setting the egg basket on a stall ledge, she stepped closer. "May I pet him?"

"Sure."

She stuck her hand out for the animal to sniff and then ran her fingers along his soft jaw and neck. The pleasant smell and feel of warm horseflesh flashed her back to childhood on Matheson Ranch.

Leaning her cheek against Huck's shoulder, she hugged his neck.

Wilder, who'd gone into the tack room, returned with a bucket of grooming tools. When he saw her hugging his horse, his mouth curved. Without saying anything, he handed her a brush and took another for himself. In silent tandem they brushed the animal.

With each stroke, Taylor's tense shoulders relaxed, the knot in her throat eased.

Occasionally, Wilder murmured something to the horse. Each time the animal pricked his ears and turned soft, adoring eyes on his owner.

Poppy always said you could tell a lot about a man by the way he treated his animals.

Wilder treated his well.

The notion gave Taylor an interesting sense of comfort, an emotion completely out of sync with the fact that he was kicking her to the curb soon. Not that she blamed him. This was trouble of her making, not his.

She still thought it was weird that he owned a ranch that he visited only a few times a year.

"Why do you pay a mortgage on a place you rarely see?"

Wilder's brush clattered into the silver metal bucket. He patted the horse's hip. "You're good to go, boy. Thanks for the ride."

Seeming to understand, Huck ambled with soft clops down the alley and out into the sunlit corral.

As if she hadn't spoken, the cowboy gathered a long rope and began coiling it in wide loops. Feeling ignored but, considering the grace period for moving that he'd given her, she didn't ask again.

Toting the bridle and reins, she was halfway inside the tack room when Wilder spoke.

"A man needs a place to come home to. Someplace that's his that no one can ever take away."

Something in his soft, rusty voice struck a chord deep inside Taylor's soul. She heard heartache and longing. Surely there was a painful story behind those few words.

She stepped out to look at him.

With his head down, white hat low, his expression was unreadable.

"You're right, though," he went on. "I'm not here much. Nearly five months on the road this time and more to come for me to get a shot at the finals. Seems a shame to let the place sit empty."

She couldn't disagree. "It's a wonderful home."

As eager as she was to travel again and keep her blog lucrative, she liked it here.

He cleared his throat, his hands continuing to slide along the white, flexible rope. Thick fingers, strong and sure.

"Someday I'll retire from the circuit to raise and train roping horses here. That's what the half-built building is for." He motioned toward the structure she'd wondered about. "But that's someday. Next weekend I'm back on the road."

She would be too, though not in the footloose, traveling, adventuresome way she loved.

"So," he said, "I've been praying."

He'd told her that already. "Did God talk back?"

She was halfway teasing, halfway not. Poppy claimed the Lord spoke to him. Not in an audible voice but through inner nudgings and the Bible. As much as she wasn't interested in religion, she knew Poppy didn't lie. She, on the other hand, had never heard a word from God. His actions spoke louder than any words ever could.

"Actually, I think He did." His nervous movements on the rope stilled and he looked up at her from beneath his hat brim. "You asked me about a housekeeping job."

"Yes." Her pulse sped up.

"You've taken good care of the place. Improved it, even."

Was he going to let her stay? "I tried."

"You did. Even though I'm not much on goats or chickens."

"I'll have to sell them anyway when I leave, and I'll take down the pens so they're not a bother."

"They're not. What I mean is—" he swallowed "—you're in a bad spot."

Thanks, Cowboy Obvious. "I can take care of myself."

"Understood. You've made that clear. But that baby you're carrying is my niece or nephew."

She hadn't considered that, but he was right. Half right anyway. "I suppose so."

"No *suppose* to it. I have an obligation."

The tension jumped back on her shoulders and clamped down harder than a vise.

"No. You do not."

She didn't want to be an obligation to anyone. That was part of the reason she didn't go home to her family.

Wilder stepped around her, blithely unaware that he'd pushed her worst hot button, and hung the rope inside the tack room.

With the equipment stored away and the horse happily grazing the fertile green grass, Wilder reached for the basket of eggs that she'd set aside while grooming the horse.

He started across the corral, waiting at the gate for her to catch up. When she did, he opened the wide metal enclosure and waited for her to walk through.

Courteous of him.

Taylor was still trying to figure out the point of his conversation.

Slowing his boot steps to match hers, he walked her to the back door, opened it and set the eggs inside.

He turned back to her. "You planted a garden."

She was expecting more of his obligation talk. "I thought I'd be here all summer."

"Will you show it to me? Your animals too."

Was he going to offer to buy them? If so, who would care for them when he was away?

She shrugged and stepped off the low back step. "It's your ranch."

A smile quivered at the corners of his mouth. He was a serious man but he was easy with his smiles.

"You finally decided I'm telling the truth and that this really is my property?"

"All things considered, a lie would have made more sense." Hers certainly had. At least to her.

He laughed. "Can't argue that. Ours is a tangled-up situation, no doubt."

Tangled-up was a mild term compared to the complicated catastrophe Cale Gadsden had caused. For her, her baby and for Wilder.

Wilder could pray all day if he wanted to, but even God couldn't untangle the mess she'd made.

Chapter Five

Like the rest of his place, Taylor's chicken house and adjacent wire pen were neatly put together, though she'd mostly used scrap lumber and odds and ends from the storage shed she'd thought was Cale's.

"Nice," he said, running his fingertips along the chicken wire. "Where did you get the hens?"

"Jordy Fitts, except for Esther. He helped me with the pen too." At the sound of Taylor's voice, the plump chickens rushed the fence. They strutted and clucked, pecking eagerly at the ground in hopes of a treat.

"Jordy's a good man."

"You know him?"

"In an area this small? Sure. Not many people I don't know. We attend the same church."

"When you're home."

"Right." He hadn't been to his home church since Christmas. He missed it, another reason he was eager to retire and settle down. A man needed the support of a regular congregation, both for fellowship and to help hold him accountable. "Who's Esther?"

Taylor pointed to a red chicken in one corner of

the pen, squatting forlornly in a small wire cage. "She belongs to Flora Grimley."

She told him about hitting the hen with her car and Flora's reaction.

He chuckled softly. "Not funny, I know, but Flora is a tough case. I'm surprised she gave you the hen."

"I was too. I thought she'd shoot her. Or me."

"I think her bark is worse than her bite. She's just as wounded as that hen."

Each time he was home, he made an effort to befriend the woman, which meant he had to sneak over there in the early morning hours to mow her lawn or mend a fence. The result was always the same. She waited until he was finished and then ran him off with a stern warning not to come back.

He'd wave and smile as he drove away, knowing he'd return. Sooner or later, he'd wear her down.

"What makes you say she's wounded?" Taylor asked.

He twitched his shoulders in a shrug. He wasn't a know-it-all, but he understood nature.

"Angry people are usually hurt people. Take a horse, for example."

Taylor's eyes sparkled with humor. "Are you calling Flora a horse?"

He laughed as he tugged a red feather from between the six-sided fence wires and rubbed it across his palm. "Nope. Just using what I know to make a point."

"Which is?"

"A mistreated horse will fight, bite, kick and do everything he can to get rid of you. Not because he's mad at you, but because he's afraid. Fight or flight kicks in."

"I guess that's true."

"People are the same. The only way to heal a damaged horse is tenderness and patience."

Removing his hat, Wilder slid the red feather into the narrow band, all the while wrestling with his conscience. Chitchat about his grumpy neighbor and Taylor's chickens was not the conversation they needed to have.

"So you think kindness is the answer to everything?"

Now, there was a loaded question that made his conscience ping louder. He studied the small feather, rust red against the summer white straw.

"Just a feeling I have. She needs a good neighbor, a friend. I try to be one."

Turning from the chicken pen, he replaced his hat and pointed toward the small patch of plants. "Your garden?"

Pride brightened her expression. "It's not very big. I started small, but so far, everything I planted has come up."

She gave him the tour, naming each plant and pointing out the tiny green orbs that would become peppers and tomatoes.

"For salsa," she said. "I have a great recipe I learned to make on one of my trips to Mexico."

"I like salsa." He didn't know why he'd said that, except to encourage her to keep talking so he wouldn't have to. "Hot or mild?"

"Spicy, but not enough to make you sweat. Much milder than what my south-of-the-border friends prefer." She crossed her eyes and waved a hand in front of her mouth. "I'm not brave enough for the really hot stuff."

Wilder's eyes crinkled at her antics. She seemed pretty brave to him. Pregnant, alone, in a new place, and both she and the property were thriving. Plenty brave to him.

She'd worked hard, turning this unused plot of his good, rich dirt into rows of vegetables. The rows were crooked, but that didn't detract from the healthy-looking plants or the obvious amount of effort that had gone into working the soil and planting the seeds.

If she left now, she'd never see her garden come to fruition. Or get to share her favorite salsa.

The pressure to mount a white horse and ride to her rescue grew with each breath.

Sometimes he didn't know the difference between his will and the Lord's.

This was one of those times.

Was his overactive sense of responsibility ousting his good sense? He didn't even know this woman.

Or was the Lord urging him to step out of his comfort zone and become a Good Samaritan for the sake of someone in need?

Taylor. And a tiny relative he'd yet to meet.

Resentment toward his half brother curdled in his chest. Nothing good had ever come from knowing his paternal family. Nothing.

As soon as the thought came, he felt a check in his spirit. The baby Taylor carried, Cale's baby, was pure and innocent and good, exactly the way God created every child to be. He or she had no say in their parentage.

"Girl or boy?"

Taylor, bending to pluck a weed from the tomato plants, raised her face toward him. "Boy. Why?"

With the morning sun around her like golden halos, she looked wholesome and pretty working in her garden. Her garden, not his. She'd put in the work.

"Just curious. I keep thinking about him and didn't know whether to think *him* or *her.*"

She straightened, a hand to her back, smiling at his convoluted thought process. "Now you know. A boy. I haven't thought of a name yet." She made a face. "Definitely not after his father."

"Can't argue that." He crouched on his boot toes and plucked a few weeds for her.

"Why are you thinking about my baby?"

His chest tightened. Good question.

Just spit it out. Say it. It's the right thing to do.

He hoped so. He surely hoped so.

"Doesn't seem right for you not to make that salsa." He flicked his eyes up and then back down.

She stood above him, a few feet away. Her belly protruded, reminding him again why he had to do this.

"I was thinking the same thing," she said. "I'll miss this place, my garden, the chickens, Veronica."

He frowned, tossed a handful of moist-rooted weeds out of the vegetable patch and pushed to a stand. "Who's Veronica?"

"My nanny goat. She's a sweetheart."

The only goats he'd encountered were obnoxious, head-butting little monsters. He was not a fan. "A billy goat once knocked me over a fence."

She held back a snort, laughing eyes scanning his strong, sturdy body. "Sorry, that seems impossible."

"I was six. A pint-sized six."

"Veronica is very mild-tempered. I could never have learned to milk her otherwise."

Again he was impressed. She'd learned to build a chicken pen and milk a goat. What other skills did this interesting woman have?

"So, what about it?" he asked.

Blue eyes blinked at him. "What about what?"

"I don't have time to milk a goat or care for a garden. I won't even be here to gather the eggs. And I know nothing about making salsa." He waved a hand over the garden and toward the chicken pen. "You can't leave me to handle all this unfinished business."

"You want me to stay?"

The hope in her expression finished him off.

Hedging a teeny bit, he held out a hand. "Temporarily. Wouldn't hurt to have someone keep an eye on things while I'm gone. With all the work to do around here now, I can't afford to hire someone else. If you're willing to take care of the place for room and board, we might work something out. Temporarily."

He drew in a deep breath of morning air, prayed like mad he wasn't making a colossal mistake and blurted, "You want to house-sit for me?"

Taylor had never wanted to hug someone so badly in all her life. So she did.

And knocked off his hat.

Theirs was an awkward hug, her belly in the way, and they both jerked back to laugh uncomfortably.

"I guess you accept?" he asked.

"Yes. Thank you. Thank you." She sounded breathless because she was. Breathless with relief. "I won't forget this kindness and I promise to take exquisite care of your property."

A flush crested his cheekbones, darkening his already tanned skin. "I know you will. You already have."

She didn't know what had caused Wilder's swift change of mind but if it was his prayer, she owed God a thank-you. And maybe an apology.

"Just until the baby comes," she clarified. "I write a travel blog so, like you, I need to be on the road ASAP or lose my sponsorships."

"You make a living writing a blog?" Wilder retrieved his hat from the moist garden dirt and dusted it against his jeans.

She wiped her hands down the leg of her shorts, aware that she'd probably wiped most of the dirt on the back of Wilder's shirt. "You make a living throwing a rope?"

He grinned. "Is this where I say 'touché'? Sounds like we both have unusual careers. But I'm serious. I didn't know a person could earn a living writing blogs."

Lately, that living wasn't so great.

"I'll show you sometime. Or you can google me and see for yourself." She bit her bottom lip and admitted, "Right now, the blog is struggling a little." Or rather, she was.

"Why?"

"I write a *travel* blog, Wilder, and I am not currently nor for the foreseeable future going anywhere farther than my doctor's office in Centerville."

"Oh, I see your problem. Yeah." He raked a hand over the back of his muscled neck, his eyebrows pinched together in thought. "Southeastern Oklahoma is a popular travel destination. Some guy in the next town reopened a guest ranch. My buddy, Pate, lives over that way and says it's a nice one. Persimmon Hill, I think the new place is called. You could drive over there, spend a day and write about that."

No, she couldn't. Not there.

"I've written about a dude ranch before." Not that she couldn't write about a different one, just not *that* one.

Too bad really. It was a great idea. But Persimmon Hill was off-limits for the time being.

It belonged to her sister's fiancé.

A man shouldn't be uncomfortable in his own home. But Wilder was.

For two days he found things to do outside. He worked on the new horse facilities. He'd even cleaned the shed as well as the old cellar he never used, two jobs he'd put off for months. Years.

This morning, he'd taken a load of trash to the city dump and mucked out Taylor's chicken pen, storing the free fertilizer in a fifty-gallon drum.

When he could think of nothing else to do, he'd gone inside the house to wash a load of laundry.

The machine was already in use. By Taylor.

He couldn't complain. His towels had never smelled better or felt softer.

However, as soon as he'd made the decision to let her live in his house, he was faced with a bigger dilemma.

She was living in his house. Physically living in his house.

Which meant he couldn't. Or rather, he wouldn't.

Call him strait-laced or old-fashioned, but living with a woman meant marriage first. His mother had drilled that into his head using her own painful experience—and his—as an example. Out of respect for Taylor, himself and the Lord, he continued to spend his nights in his trailer. He already lived there most of the time when on the rodeo circuit, so sleeping in the camper wasn't that big of a deal.

Besides, Scripture was adamant about steering clear of temptation. He knew this because last night he'd spent an hour googling Scripture references. One that stuck in his head was now posted on the tiny bathroom mirror in the even tinier washroom of his RV.

Watch and pray, that ye enter not into temptation: the spirit indeed is willing, but the flesh is weak.

Wilder thought his flesh was pretty strong but he was taking no chances.

He wanted to be on solid ground with the Lord, but he was also confident God wanted him to look after Taylor. He just had to be careful how he went about it.

Not that he was tempted. Certainly not by a woman who was seven months pregnant with his half sibling's baby. He just didn't want to be.

So his camper remained his home on wheels.

Better, but not perfect.

He was still aware of Taylor Matheson.

She was no problem. It wasn't that. The place looked cleaner, tidier, better than he'd ever seen it. She insisted on cooking for him. He sure wouldn't complain about that. Last night, she'd made a dish from an internet recipe. John Wayne Casserole. He could get on board with ground beef and cheese any day of the week. He'd eaten half the pan. And enjoyed having someone else to talk to during the meal.

Taylor was a pleasant woman. Conversation was easy, though they kept things light as strangers do.

So what was it? Why did he feel uncomfortable?

He figured he knew the answer. Even though he spent his nights in the camper and most of his awake time outside, they still shared the house. He came and went as if he owned the place.

As the thought crossed his mind, he snorted. He *did* own the place. She was the stranger, although she behaved as if she, not he, belonged there.

Theirs was a conundrum.

"Lord," he muttered to the lid of the whirring washing machine, "what have You gotten me into?"

When the Lord didn't answer, Wilder stashed his trash bag of dirty clothes in the hall closet.

He peeked around the kitchen door. She was in there.

Going to the fridge, he poured himself a glass of leftover tea.

Taylor looked up from what appeared to be a high school science project and grinned behind huge plastic safety goggles.

He hitched his chin and wandered into the living room.

What in the world was she doing?

Not his business. She'd live her life. He'd live his. Strictly a compassionate business arrangement for the sake of his nephew. Easier that way.

He was accustomed to being alone at home after being surrounded by people for days on end. He required the solitude to rest and gear up for the next round of rodeos.

Every time he prayed about the situation, hoping another solution would come to mind, he became more confident that this was the right thing and more aware that the child she carried was his kin. With only one other blood relative on the planet that he knew of—the biological father who'd rejected him—Wilder felt a certain kinship with the baby. A responsibility.

There was that word again. Responsibility.

Taylor had made it clear in their negotiations that she was an independent woman who needed neither his help nor a caregiver. She would work for him in exchange for a place to stay until the baby came. He was not responsible.

The alarm on his internal meter shot off the scale. He still *felt* responsible.

With an inward groan, Wilder settled in his favorite recliner and tried watching a few roping videos.

Unable to concentrate because of the pregnant stranger puttering around in his kitchen in rubber gloves and safety goggles, he tossed the remote aside and left the house.

Halfway to his truck, key already in hand, he stopped on the green grass.

Should he tell her where he was going?

Or not.

He owed her no explanation. He wasn't responsible.

That word again.

He tilted his head back and blew a troubled breath at the puffy white clouds.

Driving away without a word seemed rude. What if she needed something from town? Although his ranch was only two miles west of Mercy, why should she make the trip if he was already going? Gas wasn't cheap anymore. And he hadn't a clue if she had adequate money.

She wrote a travel blog and she wasn't traveling.

Was she pressed for cash? Did she need to buy things for the baby? So far, he'd seen little evidence of a prepared nursery.

Should he offer to pay her for taking care of the house?

With a beleaguered, troubled groan, he marched back inside the house and into the kitchen.

She'd removed the gloves and goggles. The plastic glasses left deep pink imprints on her cheeks. Instead of detracting, they looked cute. She looked cute. Round as a turtle but still cute.

The counter was littered with pots and spoons and various containers of unknown substances. The whole house smelled like flowers.

"I'm going into Mercy. Do you need anything?" He sounded grumpy because he was.

"I can go later. Don't bother."

"If I asked, it's not a bother."

"You sound as if it's a bother." She bit her bottom lip. "Did I do something wrong?"

His conscience jabbed him. "No."

"Are you regretting your decision?"

"No!" Yes. "Do you need anything from town or not?"

"Not."

This wasn't going well.

Wilder held up both hands and blew out a gusty breath. "I'm sorry. This is such a weird situation. I'm not sure how to act."

"Act naturally, maybe?"

He allowed a half chuckle. "There is nothing natural about having my estranged half brother's pregnant ex-girlfriend that I don't even know living under my roof while I live in my horse trailer."

"I still don't understand that, Wilder. Why not share the house with me? It's not like we're together."

It would actually have been better if they were.

Then this whole confused calamity would make sense. "People will talk."

"They will anyway."

"But my conscience will be clear. I don't want people thinking the wrong thing about us. About you."

"This isn't the eighteenth century, Wilder. Couples live together all the time. No one thinks anything about it."

He did. "We're not a couple."

"That's not my point. We can be housemates, sharing this comfortable home."

Wilder crossed both arms over his chest. "No."

Taylor gazed at him for a long moment. Then, she turned away and began clearing off the counter. "You're the boss. I'll clean this up."

He'd hurt her feelings.

He dropped his arms to his sides and watched her. Maybe he should just leave. He was entered in a rodeo this weekend. He could leave now, stay at Pate's or Jess's place for a couple of days, rope a lot of practice steers, tune up a bit.

He had to earn some money points at every rodeo or lose his standing. Dangling at the cutoff mark, number fifteen, was a dangerous spot. If one guy did better or Wilder did worse, he could lose this one shot at the National Finals he'd worked for all these years. Most cowboys never made the finals. Though the most crucial days of the rodeo season were just getting started, this was the first time he'd been this close to the big show. He had to make every event count. No cowboy was guaranteed a second shot.

But he couldn't leave behind hurt feelings. Mama always said an apology helped him as much as the injured party. Friend and mentor, Jess Beamer would tell him to mend his fences before it was too late and the cows got out.

Their advice had never failed him.

"What are you making?" His words weren't an apology, but they were a start.

Taylor was always making something. He'd never seen a woman as busy with crafts and creative ideas.

And strange science experiments.

"Lavender soap. Since the last batch turned out perfectly, I'm making another. I'll sell them both at the store."

Her voice had lost its energy. She didn't look at him.

He rotated his shoulders.

Do the right thing even when you don't want to.

He could practically hear Jess's voice in his ear. Jess, the man who'd taken Wilder in when his mother died. Father figure, friend and mentor, Jess Beamer had taught him to rodeo, to pray and to be a man.

Doing right was Jess's mantra.

It had become his own.

"Taylor."

"What?"

Wilder scratched the back of his neck and wished she'd turn around and look at him. "Why not come with me to the store? You can sell your soap and eggs, save a trip."

"No, thank you. I'll go later."

Yep. He'd hurt her feelings.

"I'd enjoy the company."

She turned around then, eyes bright. "Liar."

Had she been about to cry?

"Come with me. I'll wait until you finish this. Or better yet, I'll help you. Okay?" He intentionally kept his voice as kind and apologetic as possible.

A look of pleasure mixed with considerable relief flashed at him. Had she been as tense as he? Had she been worried that he'd grow tired of the camper and send her packing?

Probably. Which made him feel like a jerk. His intent was to help her, not make her miserable.

Do the right thing.

His kitchen wasn't large and he was, but he eased up to the counter next to her. "Show me what to do."

"I'm almost finished."

"Fine. I'll clean up."

"You don't need to do that. I'm the housekeeper. I want to earn my keep, remember?"

A lock of brown hair had pulled loose from her ponytail. Wilder resisted the urge to loop it behind her ear.

"Takes some getting used to."

"In more ways than one, I imagine." She turned to face him. "I don't want you to feel miserable."

"Am I making you uncomfortable?"

She slid the goggles and gloves into a kitchen drawer. The one where he'd kept his necessary junk. Hammer, screws, twine, glue, duct tape and bits of other junk he didn't know what to do with but might need for something. What had she done with those?

"On my travels," she said, turning toward him with her back against the counter, "I've slept in hostels, spare rooms, B and Bs, on trains, in tents under the stars and about anywhere else you can think of. I'm only uncomfortable because you are, Wilder. And I hate that. Why not let me live in the camper and work for you during the day?"

"No." What kind of thoughtless jerk would he be to relegate a woman, a *pregnant* woman, to a small travel trailer with rudimentary facilities?

"I'll be comfortable there," she insisted.

Wilder snorted. "No, you won't. We've had this conversation before. I need my trailer. I'll be heading out early in the morning. No sense in you moving back and forth between house and camper. I'm used to it."

Wilder added a handful of utensils to the dishwasher, something else in his house that he rarely used. When a man lived alone, he used one of each item. One plate, one glass, one fork. Washing up was easy.

Taylor apparently loved the dishwasher. She'd even bought dishwasher pods, something he'd never bothered with.

When the kitchen was orderly again, she disappeared down the hall while he carried the eggs and a box of sweet-scented soap squares to his truck.

He started the engine and waited. He didn't have to wait long. She came out wearing a flowered sundress, a small yellow bag over her shoulder.

Pretty as a garden of sunflowers.

He hopped out of the truck to open the passenger door and steadied Taylor as she stepped up and in.

Her gentle fragrance stirred around them and found its way into his nostrils and his brain. A brain that said Taylor Matheson was a lovely woman.

Back in the driver's seat, Wilder pulled onto the road and tried not to resent the man who'd caused him and Taylor so much trouble.

His half brother was not only cruel, he was stupid.

Chapter Six

Oh, no. She'd fouled up again. Maybe her sisters were right. Maybe she *did* need a keeper.

First, she'd married the wrong man. Or thought she had. Then, she'd moved into the wrong man's house. And now this.

Taylor fidgeted with the blocks of scented soap, suddenly, *painfully*, aware that she hadn't told Wilder everything he needed to know before they walked into the Mercy Mercantile.

He'd already been irritated at her this morning. She didn't want to infuriate him.

As he pulled into the graveled parking lot outside the town's only general purpose store and killed the engine, she turned toward him. "Uh, Wilder."

About to exit the vehicle, he paused, key in hand. "Yes?"

"I need to tell you something before you go inside."

Curiosity shadowed his eyes. "Okay. Shoot."

"Promise you won't be mad?"

He huffed a short laugh. "You sound ten years old."

Turning one of the soap bars round and round in her hands, she admitted, "I've made a lot of mistakes. One of them was believing anything Cale told me, including the lie about your ranch."

"I already know about that." His tone was gentle, kind, as if he sympathized. She supposed he did. He really was a nice guy. Which gave her hope that he wouldn't be furious. Or dump her out on the gravel and drive away without a backward glance.

"What you don't know is this. I told that same story to the people of Mercy. They think my husband died and I'm now a widow, living on his ranch, awaiting the birth of his child."

Sometimes a white lie came back to bite her. This was one of those times.

Wilder's expression, heretofore curious, flattened. "Are you saying that Walt and Milly think I'm dead? And that I'm your dead husband and this is my baby?"

She hunched deeper and deeper into the cushions, feeling small enough to crawl under the seat.

"Probably." Her voice squeaked. "I mean, they know you. They know you own that ranch. They know I've been living there for the past few months and you've been nowhere around. I didn't exactly name names."

"So, they've jumped to the wrong conclusion." He scrubbed a hand over his face hard enough to redden his nose. "Man."

"I'm sorry. I keep making the problem worse."

"You'll have to tell them the truth."

Poppy always said the truth would set you free.

He was wrong this time. The truth was going to choke her. "I know."

"It's going to be embarrassing."

"I know."

"Okay." He patted her tense fingers and reached for his door handle. "I'll go with you. Let's get it over with."

Twilight zone, Wilder thought. Either that or one of those reality TV shows where people embarrass themselves for money while the whole world watches.

A couple of people were getting gas at the pumps next door, but inside the Mercantile was quiet. A lanky kid carrying a can of Mountain Dew and a bag of Flamin' Hot Cheetos came out as Wilder and Taylor entered.

The old-fashioned wood interior smelled of cleaner and klobase, a kind of specialty Czech sausage Walt made from his grandfather's recipe. He must be stirring up a batch today. Wilder wouldn't leave here without a package of sausage wrapped in white butcher paper and ready to eat with a cheese round from Walt's cheddar wheel.

First, there was a problem Taylor had to fix.

She'd done this. She could tell the tale.

He was only here for moral support.

But he'd stand with her. No use being a worse jerk than his half brother.

The bell over the door jangled. Milly glanced

up from behind a counter, glasses on the edge of her nose. She slowly removed them, her expression going from friendly interest to shock.

"Wilder Littlefield?" she asked, incredulous. "Is that you?"

Wilder removed his hat. "Yes, ma'am."

Milly hustled around the end of the old-fashioned butcher block counter and threw her arms around him.

After a brief hug, she pushed him back, but didn't release him. That was Milly. At around sixty years old, with straight, chopped, gray hair and a big heart, she and Walt were good folks who made everyone entering the store feel like family.

Considering the size of the town, half of them were.

Face filled with delight and wonder, the rosy-cheeked Milly gave his shoulders a shake. "Let me look at you. You scoundrel. We thought you were dead."

Wilder shifted uncomfortably. "I know."

Milly whipped around and bellowed, "Walt, get out here. The dead have risen."

Walt, drying his hands on a white dish towel, quickly emerged from behind a curtained doorway, a look of bewilderment on his face. When he spotted Wilder, his reaction matched that of his wife. Wonder. Thrill. Surprise.

Wilder experienced a mix of pleasure and embarrassment. They were glad he wasn't dead. Really glad. There was something kind of nice about that.

"Boy, boy, boy." Walt, tossing the towel on the counter, rushed to him, clasping his hand in a firm shake. "Our hearts broke when your sweet little wife told us you were gone."

"Um, about that." Wilder turned toward his companion, who, up to this moment, had remained hidden behind him. "Taylor. This is where you come in."

Complexion pale, she cleared her throat. "Milly. Walt. There's been a bit of a misunderstanding."

"We're sure glad of it too, honey," Milly said. "We're tickled pink to know our Wilder is alive and kicking."

"That's not the misunderstanding I meant. I'm glad he's alive too, but he's not him. I mean—" Clearly struggling, Taylor clutched the box of scented soap to her chest. "I mean—Wilder is not my husband."

Wonder changed to confusion on the faces of both storekeepers. Milly's gaze fell to Taylor's midsection. "But hon, you're having his baby."

Heat burned up the sides of Wilder's face. This was what he'd been concerned about. But he kept quiet, letting Taylor take the reins.

"No, ma'am. I'm not. I mean, I'm having a baby but—it's a long story." Her fingers, white as goat milk, trembled against the cardboard soap box she'd perched on top of the baby in question. "I'm sorry. I messed everything up and lied to you but I didn't mean to lie. Well, not completely."

"You lied about him dying?"

"No, not that. I thought he'd died. I mean, he *did* die. But not Wilder."

She was confusing even Wilder, and he knew the story.

His sympathy gene was acting up again. Maybe he should go to the truck and leave her to handle it.

He wouldn't. Couldn't. The other gene, the responsibility one, was also on high alert.

Milly, the talker of the pair, looked from Taylor to Wilder. "I don't understand. If Wilder didn't die, who did?"

Taylor blushed a deep red. Her lips quivered. She blinked blue eyes.

Rapidly.

Glassy, moist eyes.

Oh, man.

The small hint of tears was Wilder's undoing. As usual.

"Milly. Walt." He stepped in front of Taylor, took the box of soap and set it on the counter. "This was a case of mistaken identity. Taylor thought my ranch belonged to her…ex."

He stopped at the term *ex* without adding boyfriend or husband, determined not to lie but also determined not to embarrass her further. This was on Cale, not on her. Most of it anyway. Unless she was lying again, she'd believed she and Cale were married.

"Her ex?" Walt scratched the side of his neck. "I thought she was a widow."

"She was. Is. Sort of." He removed his hat and bounced it against his knee. The back of his neck was in a sweat. This was getting more complicated by the minute. "Let's leave it at widow, okay?"

"So this is not your baby?" Milly glanced from him to Taylor and back.

"No, ma'am." Taylor's stricken expression made Wilder almost wish it was. "But I'm relieved not to be dead."

"Thank the good Lord you're not." Milly frowned. "But who is?"

Wilder replaced his hat, and when Taylor only stared at him with wide blue eyes and didn't answer, he did.

"My brother."

The couple's troubled expressions turned to sympathy faster than the internet posted Taylor's blogs. Though still on the hot seat, Taylor watched the attention turn from her mistakes to the discomfited man blocking her with his big shoulders.

"Wilder, dear boy, you must be shattered." Milly grabbed him in another hug, patting his back in comfort. "I am so sorry for your loss."

Wilder, looking about as mortified as she felt, dipped his head. "Thank you. He was my half brother, and we weren't close, but his death was a shock."

He'd insisted she be the one to do the telling, but he'd stepped in and covered for her. Taylor didn't know whether to thank him or punch him.

She could handle herself. She didn't need him or her sisters or anyone else to run her life.

Except lately she hadn't been doing such a great job.

All the more reason to keep her distance from Matheson Ranch and work harder at proving herself.

She had to admit Wilder's input had relieved a load of stress. Walt and Milly were good people who'd treated her well, helped her get established and even gave her credit at the store until her eggs and crafts sold. She didn't want them to distrust her or to think she was some kind of immoral con woman the way Wilder had at first.

Milly reached out to take Taylor's hand, holding it between both of hers. "Our precious Taylor, all alone without her man, still grieving but determined to stiffen her spine and make a life for that baby all by herself." She gave Taylor's fingers a squeeze. "Hon, grief can cause anyone to make mistakes. No wonder you thought Wilder's ranch belonged to your husband. Pregnant and alone, widowed, in a fog of grief. You are about as brave and strong as they come."

Taylor wasn't feeling brave or strong. She felt

like a lying, dishonest, useless pile of junk who'd misled the good people of this town. But she *had* been all of Milly's other descriptors when she'd arrived at Three Nails Ranch.

Well, except the widowed.

Somehow Milly had glossed right over the fact that Wilder had avoided claiming Cale as her husband. Taylor was grateful. One humiliation was enough for today. She didn't want to explain that horrific error in judgment to anyone ever again.

"Milly, you and Walt and the people of Mercy have made these past few months easier with your kindness and generosity. I will always be grateful."

"Honey, the pleasure was all ours. You're a fine addition to our little hole-in-the-road town. You've got the ladies clamoring for your crafts, and that blog of yours is the talk of the town."

Sadly, she'd probably continue to be the talk of the town, although not in the way she'd like. The Mercantile was the unofficial news center of Mercy, Oklahoma. Walt and Milly would tell the tale, which, come to think of it, was better than having to tell it herself.

Taylor slid her gaze to Wilder. His tanned skin was dark with embarrassment, but he seemed doggedly determined to support her. Why would he do that? They barely knew each other.

What kind of man stood up for a stranger who'd caused him nothing but trouble?

Certainly not Cale Gadsden.

But, apparently, Cale's brother was cut from a different cloth.

A man who took serious the old-fashioned role of protector, defender, provider.

Right down to inconveniencing himself.

She didn't want Wilder to be her benefactor, didn't want a defender or a keeper. For four years she'd proven to herself that she could be an independent woman, handling her own problems.

But, today, just for today, she was glad to have the broad-shouldered cowboy by her side.

I nearly died of embarrassment. Wilder had always heard people say that, but now he thought it could happen.

He'd been embarrassed before—especially during a roping event when he'd completely missed the calf and scored a no-time—but this was different.

When he'd invited Taylor to ride into town with him, he'd been doing so as an apology. He should have thought things through first. He never considered that he was supposed to be dead.

Wilder exited the Mercantile and pulled his truck to the gas station next door while Taylor remained inside to sell her eggs and soap and do a bit of shopping.

A car pulled in at the next pump. A man got out, saw him and exclaimed, "Wilder! You're alive."

Here he went again.

Repocketing his credit card, he crossed the median to shake hands with Charlie Lavigne.

"The rumors of my death are greatly exaggerated," he joked, paraphrasing Mark Twain's famous words.

"What happened? How did such a wild rumor get started?"

"Long story." He was about to switch topics to Charlie's almost famous watermelon patch when Taylor came waddling across the gravel, toting two paper sacks. Wilder nodded his head toward Charlie. "Excuse me a second."

Boots crunching gravel, he hurried to take the bags from her and received a grateful smile for his efforts. Given the situation, he didn't feel much like smiling back, but hers was nice to look at.

As they walked together down the incline to his truck, or rather, as he walked and Taylor waddled, Taylor placed a hand on his elbow.

"Sorry," she murmured. "I'm a little unbalanced."

Wilder shifted the bags to one arm, giving her full access to the crook of his elbow. "Don't fall."

Wilder could feel Charlie's gaze on them.

His stomach sank.

When they reached the truck and Wilder assisted the too-pregnant-to-make-the-climb Taylor into the passenger seat, Charlie spoke up.

"You ain't dead, but looks like the rest is true.

You got married and are gonna be a daddy. Congratulations."

Wilder sighed, removed the nozzle from the truck and hung it on the pump. "Charlie, there's been a big misunderstanding. Taylor is my brother's—her baby is my nephew, my brother's child."

There. The truth. Maybe not the whole truth, but Taylor and her baby, and even her presence at his ranch, was no one's business but his.

"Your brother died? And you've taken in his widow?"

"Something like that." He didn't want to sound like a hero when he was about as reluctant as a man could be.

Charlie left his tank to fill and clapped a hand on Wilder's shoulder. "Sorry for your loss, man. And hers. You're a good Christian for helping her out. Your brother would be proud."

Nope. Not even close. And the admission that his biological family didn't care if he lived or died still bothered him more than he wanted it to.

He didn't want to be upset with Taylor, but man, she'd put him in a bad spot.

"Thanks, Charlie. Tough times, but we're doing okay." What else could he say at this point? "So how's the melon patch this year? Gonna have any cantaloupe?"

Charlie cast one sympathetic look toward the cab of Wilder's truck before launching into a tirade against deer and raccoons that wouldn't leave his melons alone.

Wilder half listened as he finished filling his tank and looked forward to tomorrow when he, Huck and his home-away-from-home could head to the big rodeo in Texas and put Mercy, his pregnant housekeeper and all the embarrassing confusion behind them.

Chapter Seven

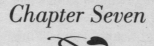

The ranch was quiet without him.

Two days after Wilder left for the next rodeo, Taylor opened the chicken pen gate, her flock clucking around her feet in eager anticipation of breakfast. She scattered a handful of the layer feed recommended by Walt on the ground to distract them while she filled their auto-feeder.

From the barn, Veronica bleated to be milked, eager to roam free to graze and generally get into things she shouldn't.

Wilder disliked goats. And goat milk. But he hadn't insisted she get rid of either. He had, however, purchased a carton of cow's milk for himself.

Different strokes, she thought. Maybe she could blog about that.

Frowning, she waded through the dozen chickens and considered the blog issue. She'd lost another affiliate sponsor yesterday.

Depressing. Worrisome.

She needed to return her sister's phone call. Another worry. She'd call without video chat, of course. Unless she kept the phone above her waist. She could do that.

The morning settled around her, empty and silent except for the animal noises.

She'd never been bothered by the solitude before. The remote ranch had been a nice break from her active lifestyle on the go.

She'd been relieved when Wilder loaded the handsome horse into his trailer and rattled down the driveway toward his next destination, taking his discomfiture with him.

She had the whole place to herself again.

Which was now the problem.

In the short while Wilder had been home, she'd enjoyed having human companionship again. Never mind that they made each other uncomfortable. She was a social person, a world traveler. She'd only become a hermit to lick her wounds and figure out what to do after the Cale debacle and until after the baby arrived.

She enjoyed having a friend, if she could call him that, to share a meal with or taste her latest cooking experiment from the internet and tell her if the result was good or just okay, which meant it was awful. Wilder was honest that way. And it didn't hurt that he was nice to look at across the table. Or that she liked watching him in the corrals, while he practiced for his next event.

Wilder, however, had seemed more than eager to hit the road and leave her and her cooking and goat milk behind.

In other circumstances, his eagerness would

have hurt her feelings. But she understood. He had a house but slept in his horse trailer. As far as he was concerned, he might as well not be here at all.

Going to Esther's cage, she lifted the little hen out to rebandage the leg. Something white rolled to one corner.

"Esther! You laid an egg." And Flora Grimley had wanted to eat the poor bird.

Thrilled, Taylor picked up the still-warm egg, considering.

She knew exactly what to do with Esther's treasure. Sneaking over there to put the egg on Flora's porch would be an adventure.

She might even blog about it.

Tired but pleased, Wilder collected his prize money at the pay office. These days, a lot of the cowboys transacted payments and entry fees online, but he liked the look and feel of money in hand. One more hint that he was getting old.

"Good roping this weekend, Wilder." The blonde cowgirl typed something on her computer and studied the screen. "Looks like you're hanging in there at number fifteen."

Fifteen. Still on the bubble. He'd hoped to make his move up in the standings this weekend but, thanks to his houseguest, his head hadn't been in the game as much as usual. He'd done okay, just not better.

He hoped she was all right by herself. Didn't

seem safe for a pregnant woman to be alone out in the country far from a hospital with the nearest neighbor being Flora Grimley.

Taylor's choice, though.

Except it wasn't, not completely, because of his irresponsible half sibling.

A hand clamped onto his shoulder. "Some of the other guys are getting together. Want to grab a bite?"

His stomach clenched, empty. He never ate before a competition. A thick steak afterward sounded amazing.

He shook his head at the other cowboy. "Nah, Wes, I'm going to grab a couple hours shut-eye and then hit the road. Thanks, though."

Another rodeo awaited him. After that, he'd head north to events in Guthrie, then Kansas and onward into Colorado and Wyoming.

No telling when he'd get back to Three Nails.

He needed to move up in the standings and the only way to do that was more wins at more rodeos.

"If you change your mind, we'll be at The Wildhorse."

He waved his friend away, pocketed his money and went to the cowboys' parking lot.

Inside his camper, he wolfed down a sandwich from his tiny fridge and pondered the long drive to Guthrie. With Pate heading back home to watch his kid play baseball in a big tournament, the gas bill for the trip would eat into this weekend's winnings.

He needed that money.

Maybe he should head back home too. Wouldn't hurt to check in on his housekeeper. Mesquite had a good-paying event coming up next weekend. It was closer to home. Instead of heading north, he could remain in Texas. Competition was stiff, but if he won, the payout was good.

He wouldn't lose his standing by missing one rodeo. Or three.

He'd check in with Taylor and, once confident she was safe, his mind would be clear and he'd rope better in Mesquite.

Removing his cell phone from his back pocket, Wilder shot Pate a text.

"Want a ride home?"

Taylor heard the rumble and rattle from the backyard. Her heart leaped. She had company. From the loud engine, her visitor was not Cindy or one of her other friends who drove puttering little cars.

Hurrying to the front yard as fast her ever-increasing bulk would allow, she watched as Wilder's huge truck, trailer in tow, pulled into the driveway.

A strange jitter stirred in her stomach. Why was he home so soon?

A thought struck. Had he been hurt? Was Huck okay?

He exited the vehicle, adjusting his hat, and went around to the back of the trailer.

"You're home," she said, and then realized she sounded like a wife or a girlfriend, instead of an interloper. "I mean, did something happen?"

Wilder opened the trailer to let Huck out.

"Yep. Old Huck and I won some money." He grinned like a proud kid, though fatigue circled his eyes. "I'm still in the running."

He'd told her about his desire to make the National Finals in Las Vegas this year for the first time in his career.

She knew enough about rodeo to ask, "How's your ranking?"

Some of the pleasure left him. "Still at fifteen."

"Hey, that's great, isn't it?"

"The bubble is not a fun place to be."

"Oh." She also knew that number sixteen got to watch the NFR on TV, not from the back of the chutes.

"But you look good." One hand on the horse's bridle, he blushed. "I mean, you look healthy. Well. Are you?"

"I am."

"Did you see the doc?"

"My appointment is tomorrow, Wilder." She patted her tummy. "But I'm feeling great and little man is active."

"Good. Good." He dipped his chin. "Well, gotta put Huck in the lot. Let him move around. He's tired of that trailer."

Had he been worried about her? Was that why

he'd come home after three days instead of being gone for weeks as he'd said?

He shouldn't, and she'd tell him so.

As he and Huck disappeared around the side of the house, Taylor went inside and boxed up the weekend's extra eggs for Milly and this afternoon's drive into Mercy.

First, she had a visit to make, one she'd have fun sharing with her blog readers. Plus, Esther's egg was a way to make friends with her unfriendly neighbor. Or at least, break the ice.

Adventure was her middle name.

If she didn't get shot.

Before she could leave the house, Wilder tapped at the back door and stepped inside, looking about as uncomfortable as he had before leaving three days ago.

Taylor sighed.

"We're past formalities, Wilder. Just come in whenever you want to. This is your house. I don't run around looking inappropriate."

He blushed deeper but looked relieved. "Good to know. Me neither."

She laughed. "I knew that without you telling me."

His Christian light shone like a beacon around him, right down to his prudish insistence on living in his horse trailer.

A grin replaced the relief. "Everything going okay around here?"

"Yes, Wilder. If you're worrying about me, don't. I am perfectly fine. I can take care of myself and this baby, but you didn't need to drive hundreds of miles to find that out. You could have called me."

"I don't have your number."

Did that mean he would have called?

Probably. She didn't know whether to be annoyed or touched.

Instead, she held out a hand. "Give me your phone."

He did and she typed her info into his contacts.

"Now, give me yours," he said. "In case you need anything."

"I won't." But she handed him the phone.

"You might. What if the house caught fire from your science experiments or you blew up the lab— aka my kitchen."

She chuckled at his humor. "True. Goat soap is a dangerous thing, and according to my family, I am a loose cannon."

She hadn't intended to mention her family but Wilder didn't seem to notice.

His eyebrow hiked. "You didn't buy a cannon, did you? I'm not sure the chickens would appreciate the noise. On the other hand, maybe the goat would run away. A man can always hope."

Taylor's laugh went deeper. She held her tummy, enjoyed the moment. "You're a funny dude, Wilder Littlefield." When he wasn't so uptight. "Sit down over there and let me fix you a half dozen of these fresh eggs."

To be honest, she was happy to see him and glad for the company.

"Sounds good, but I can fix them."

She glared at him. He backed away, grinning, both hands aloft in surrender. They'd had this conversation for a full week. She was working for her keep. He was not her sugar daddy.

Since she wasn't drinking coffee these days, Taylor poured a glass of cow's milk for Wilder, sniffed to test the freshness and set it on the table.

"You were headed somewhere," he said. "Am I holding you up?"

Taylor cracked egg after egg against the skillet and set them to sizzle while she popped toast in the toaster.

"Esther laid an egg. I'm going to give it to Flora."

"Living dangerously." He went to the fridge's upper freezer and took out the spicy sausage left from their trip last week to the Mercantile.

She tried to take the package from him, but he was bigger and stronger and bumped her gently out of the way to slice the frozen meat into rounds that he dumped into the skillet with the eggs.

The savory scent rose with the sudden sizzle and steam.

"I'll go with you."

"I don't need a protector."

"Understood. I'm going anyway."

"Determined to win her over?"

Wilder gave her a look she couldn't decipher and said, "Something like that."

She didn't believe him.

Wilder felt like an ornery kid every time he approached Flora Grimley's house. This morning, although he needed more sleep than last night's two hours and a short nap while Pate drove, he was secretly pleased to accompany Taylor on their shared mission to befriend the lonely old lady. He didn't examine the reasons, other than wanting to make sure Taylor was safe.

He was confident Flora was harmless—after all, he sneaked onto her property any time he was home, and she'd never even shot at him. She'd threatened but never followed through.

But he was taking no chances with Taylor and his nephew.

Nephew. The word stopped him in his tracks. He was still getting used to having a relative who might someday actually like him.

One thing for sure, nothing and no one was going to hurt that little boy.

Except he didn't have any say in the matter.

Zero. Nada.

Frowning, he cast a glance toward his nephew's mother. If the blog he'd been reading was an indicator of Taylor's strength of purpose, the fragile-looking woman was not a wimp. Nor did she expect anyone else to take care of her, even pregnant.

She'd nearly snapped his head off more than once about that.

He wondered why she was so adamant. Was it because of Cale's deception? He also wondered about her family but whenever he asked, she'd sidestep him.

Bad blood could do that. He could relate. And feel sorry for her. She really needed family right now. Too bad they'd rejected her, the way his had rejected him.

To make Wilder laugh—a real treat—Taylor insisted he drive the getaway car. Or in her case, her getaway Toyota. It wasn't as noisy as his giant pickup truck.

She had butterflies in her stomach, both from the silly little adventure and from the fact that Wilder wanted to come along.

What was that all about?

Slowly, as quietly as her little car would go, Wilder eased down Flora's driveway. The grumpy neighbor was nowhere to be seen.

Widening her eyes, Taylor grinned at her partner in crime, or in their case, partner in good deeds, one hand on the door handle. "I'm going to leave this door open, put the egg on the porch and run. Be ready to drive away as soon as I knock on her door."

One eyebrow hiked. "How fast are you?"

She glanced down. "Not fast."

"I am." He held out a hand. "Give me the carton."

"Nope." She pulled it away. Inside she'd included a full dozen eggs, with a note that one of them belonged to Esther, the one-legged chicken. "I can't blog about it if I don't do it." She handed him her phone. "You snap the photos."

"It's your funeral." A rather attractive little smile played around the corners of his mouth. The lines around his eyes crinkled.

She laughed and pointed a finger at him. "Stop. You said she wouldn't hurt a flea. She was all bluff."

He pumped his eyebrows, teasing. "So far."

A giggle seemed to settle between her chest and her throat.

Pulse jumping, she eased out of the car and walked as quickly as her bulk allowed, placed the egg carton on the porch, pecked her knuckles against the old-timey, torn screen door and, holding her belly with both hands, tried to run back to the car.

The effort proved ridiculous and mostly impossible. She slowed to a semifast walk.

By the time she reached the Toyota, she was laughing so hard, her side hurt.

Just as she threw her bulk into the passenger

seat, Flora yanked open the front door and stormed onto the porch, rifle in hand.

Taylor slammed the car door and squealed, "Go, go, go!"

Wilder threw the car in reverse, spun tires and hauled backward up the driveway like an expert getaway man.

Taylor collapsed against the side window, giggling.

When they reached the roadway, Wilder slowed to look back at the house. Then he looked at Taylor. Their eyes met. His twinkled, that rugged grin playing around his appealing mouth.

"That was fun," she said.

"Well, we're still alive."

"How did I look on my sprint across her yard?" She patted her tummy and snorted. "Future Olympian?"

And they both erupted in laughter.

When they arrived back at Three Nails Ranch, Wilder parked the car and, one arm across the steering wheel, turned toward her. His grin lingered like a pleasant memory.

"Flora's grass is overgrown. Want to sneak over at dawn tomorrow and watch what happens when I mow? No running required."

Still exhilarated from their silly adventure, she nodded. "You mow. I'll drive the getaway car."

Chapter Eight

After their first two Flora escapades, the tension between Taylor and the cowboy seemed to disappear. They were partners in "crime," sharing a kind deed that not only made them both feel good, but gave them something to laugh about together.

And they laughed a lot. And talked until they no longer seemed like strangers.

Fact was, she'd begun to know Wilder Littlefield better than she'd ever known Cale.

Wilder was pleasant company, a good man, and she realized quickly that he wasn't just a Sunday Christian. He was a man like her granddad who lived his faith.

According to Wilder, the Bible said that faith in Jesus healed broken hearts and that the way to Flora's heart was through showing her God's love through kindness.

Sometimes such God-talk bothered her, but Taylor remained quiet. Like Poppy, Wilder talked about Jesus too much and about how God had a plan for everyone if they'd just get on board with His will. A plan that included her and his nephew. Wilder's word—*nephew*. The idea that he was related to her child gave her a funny feeling. It connected them in a way she hadn't anticipated.

She still wasn't sure how she felt about that. Or about him. Although she definitely felt something.

When Wilder invited her to attend Wednesday night church services, she'd refused, claiming fatigue.

In truth, she was ashamed. She'd made such a mess of her life. Why would God want her and how could she ever trust Him after He took her parents away? If He had a plan, she didn't like it.

So she and God were at a standoff. She wondered if He cared?

Glue gun in hand, she gazed up at the ceiling above the kitchen island. "Do You? Wilder says You do, but I'm not so sure."

"Talking to yourself?"

She jumped, spinning toward the male voice. Wilder was back from the practice arena at his buddy's ranch. He practiced a lot. No wonder he was good.

"I didn't know you were here."

He eyed the glue gun she'd pointed at him and raised both hands. "I surrender."

Taylor laughed and lowered the craft tool. He was good at that. Making her laugh.

An odd little jitter moved through her.

With Wilder she felt entertained, challenged, energized in ways that surprised her.

"What do you think?" She held up the beginnings of a decorative grapevine wreath. This one was bright and cheerful with a sunflower and butterfly motif. "I'm selling them online. Milly offered to hang a few in her store too."

"Pretty."

"Thanks." She dabbed glue on a tiny orange butterfly and attached it to the yellow flower. "There's fresh lemonade in the fridge."

"Sounds good." He poured himself a glass and sat down at the small table. "How was your doctor's appointment?"

"Little man and I are progressing as expected." She scratched her nose with her shoulder. "Except Dr. Burns suggested I stop eating salt." Crossing her eyes to show her attitude about that, she lifted a flip-flop-encased foot. "Fluffy feet."

His eyebrows dipped. "Is that bad? I don't know much about babies or expectant mothers."

"Nothing to worry about, I'm sure." She began to unwind a length of blue-checked ribbon. "Weren't there any babies in your family?"

"Nope. Just my mom and me until she passed." He sipped the lemonade.

"No other family?"

"None that would claim us." He said the words in a matter-of-fact manner but there was a shadow in his eyes.

"Why? You're a great person!" She waved the ribbon in the air. "Not my business. Sorry."

"It's okay. As Mom always said, the fault was on them, not us. Nothing to be ashamed of."

"What happened? If you don't mind my nosiness."

One of those expressive eyebrows lifted. "As long as I don't end up on your blog again."

She laughed. "No one could recognize you from the back. You were all hat and boots." Broad shoulders and snug Wranglers. But she didn't add the latter.

Readers had loved the distant shot of a nicely muscled cowboy, crouched on boot toes as he repaired Flora Grimley's back fence.

No one complained that her travel destination was a farm-stay as she'd termed it, nor had they mentioned that she was not featured in any of the photos. The photos he'd taken on the egg escapade had revealed too much, so she'd opted to use pictures of him instead. A win-win.

His was the only blog this month that had generated any income.

Troublesome.

Nothing she could do about it right now. Not until she could travel again. Her puffy feet fairly itched to get moving.

"I promise," she said. "No more blogs unless I ask first." She folded the ribbon back and forth onto itself. "Tell me."

"All right, then." He sipped his lemonade, the humor leaving his expression as he swallowed and became contemplative.

"Hard to know where to start."

"At the beginning. Tell me about your mom. I imagine she was awesome." *Like you.* But she didn't say that.

"Special woman, my mom. The strongest person I've ever known. She didn't talk much about her early life, but I know it was rough. Her mother was an alcoholic who kicked her out when she was seventeen. Because of me. I arrived soon after."

"She was all by herself when you were born? No family or friends or anyone?"

Taylor was thankful she wasn't and wouldn't be alone. She kept in touch with friends by phone and email, and even had lunch with her bestie, Tansy Winchell, in Centerville a few times, although she'd sworn her friend to secrecy about the pregnancy and her whereabouts. For now.

Family was her emergency backup plan. She always had them if she really needed them. She just didn't want to need them.

Wilder's mom hadn't had that. She'd been a teenager. Any friends she'd had would have been kids too.

"Mostly, yeah. I think so. Life must have been real hard for her." He looked down at his fingers, sliding over the moist lemonade glass. "She didn't have to keep me but she did. Or even have me, for that matter. She always said I was the light and purpose of her life. A gift from God."

Taylor's hand rested on her belly. "I know what that's like."

"I guess you do, and I admire you for it. We struggled financially, had a lot of hard times. Mom worked two or three jobs at once and money was still short. But there was always joy in our house. She was my gift from God."

"That's a beautiful tribute, Wilder."

"I just regret that she had to work so hard and had so little in this life."

Taylor heard the things he didn't say. He'd been raised by a single mother without extended family to lean on. Life had probably been a lot worse than he let on.

Even though she'd lost her parents at age eight, she'd had plenty of family. Sometimes too much family, but Poppy and her sisters had always been there for her.

Wilder hadn't had that.

Her family loved her, yet she rejected them.

Guilt tried to creep in. She batted it down. This conversation wasn't about her or her mistakes or her helicopter family. It was about Wilder.

"How old were you when she died?"

"Sixteen."

"Wilder, that's heartbreaking. Both of you so young. What did you do?"

"I'd been working part-time for a rancher who attended our church. Good man. He took me in."

He pointed his lemonade at her. "I didn't tell you any of this to make you sad."

"You miss her."

"Every day. Her life here on earth was hard, but she was determined to support us without asking anyone for a dime. And she did." His lips tilted but his eyes were sad. "When I was a boy I desperately wanted to make things easier for her. I wanted to grow up fast and provide for her, but she died before I could. I regret that."

Although she wasn't surprised by his feelings, the declaration touched her to the soul.

"What about your father? He didn't help?"

He looked at her for a long moment. "Cale's father. He already had a wife and son. He didn't want us—refused to even believe I was his child. Still does. I didn't know any of that until after Mom died. I found his name on some of her papers and looked him up."

Again, she read between the lincs. He'd been rejected by his father, not once, but twice. "Oh, Wilder."

"Yeah, well, that's enough of my story. What's yours?"

Taylor turned toward the refrigerator, pretending to want more lemonade.

She didn't. But she also didn't want to admit that she had a perfectly loving family less than twenty miles away. A family who would welcome her with open arms.

There had never been a better time to tell the truth, but she wasn't ready. So she opted for a different kind of truth.

She turned with the refilled glass in hand. "You already know about my parents' accident. Don't you want to hear about Cale?" The mention of his name made her stomach ache. Not her heart, her stomach. "He didn't die in the arena."

"I know."

"You do?"

Expression compassionate, he nodded. "I didn't want to upset you by asking, so I looked online. The internet said he had a heart attack. I don't understand that."

Sweet Wilder. So considerate. "That's the official statement likely spun by his family, but it's only a half-truth. Turns out Cale cheated at everything, even bull-riding."

Wilder's eyes narrowed. "What? How?"

"He took drugs, Wilder. Mainly Adderall. He claimed a doctor prescribed it to help him recover from injury, but that was another of his lies. He used it to enhance his bull-riding skill." Taylor emitted a short huff, still embarrassed at how she'd been fooled.

"I've heard of it. Cowboys talk." He picked up his glass, set it down without drinking. "They claim it gives them an edge. Better reaction times make them faster. It's wrong. Bad for the sport and the athlete, but some use anyway."

But not Wilder. He was too honest. Unlike his half brother.

"Cale was so hyped-up that day, almost manic. He regularly guzzled energy drinks, so I didn't think much about his wild mood until he collapsed."

Taylor squeezed her eyes closed and swallowed hard, trying not to replay the scene in her mind.

Wilder reached for her hand. "Hey. No need for details. I get the picture. I'm real sorry."

"Thank you," she murmured. "Can we talk about something else now?"

A beat of silence passed. Then, with a deep inhale, Wilder glanced toward the kitchen, widening his eyes in a comical expression. "Like one of your science experiments? What is that stuff brewing on the counter anyway? If that's coffee, I'm not drinking it."

A wan smile lifted her lips. She saw what Wilder was doing. Making jokes to lighten the heavy moment.

Bless him, she thought. He's too good to be true.

Which only made her feel worse. He'd asked about her family and she'd sidestepped by making him feel sorry for her.

What kind of person had she become?

Yet, she was afraid she knew and longed to run off on another adventure where she'd be too busy to think or feel guilty.

Instead she was forced by circumstance to stay put and do some serious soul-searching.

* * *

Wilder left for Mesquite on Thursday. The drive wasn't far, but every mile he put between him and Taylor seemed like a hundred.

He was growing attached.

How could that have happened in such a short time?

Was it because of the baby, his nephew?

Or was it the spunky woman herself with her crafts and perfumy soaps and funny travel blog? She'd even posted a photo of herself in those hideous outsized safety goggles and elbow-length rubber gloves, eyes crossed like some mad scientist.

He'd loved it.

Just for laughs, he'd saved that photo to his phone's lock screen to look at every time his phone pinged.

Taylor was seven months pregnant. Alone.

That worried him. He wanted to be there to make sure she was okay.

The two-lane highway stretched long and curvy as he pulled the trailer farther and farther away from Three Nails, leaving a very pregnant woman alone in his house.

He still recalled the terror of the day he'd come home from school to find his mother too sick and delirious to recognize him. She'd died two days later.

What if something happened to Taylor while he was away?

"What are you scowling about?" From the passenger seat, Pate's voice jarred him. "We're almost there."

"Ah, nothing. Just hoping Taylor will be all right while I'm away."

"Is she sick?"

"No, Sherlock," he said with a touch of friendly sarcasm. "She's pregnant."

"When Shelby was pregnant her mom or sister stayed with her while I was rodeoing."

"Taylor doesn't have close family."

"Too bad."

"Yeah."

Pate shifted in the seat to stare at him. "You're getting mighty wrapped up in this situation. Are you sure you're not the baby's daddy?"

"Positive. My brother is. I told you that."

"Maybe that's why you worry too much."

Wilder stretched the muscles across his shoulders. "Yeah, I suppose."

Pate propped a boot on Wilder's dash and leaned his seat back. "Women have babies all the time. No big deal."

Wilder huffed a laugh. "Easy for us to say. But that's my nephew she's carrying."

"Which doesn't have much to do with you, unless you're planning on taking care of him. And her."

Wilder glared at his friend. What was he getting at? "She's single, alone, about to have a baby. I know what that's like."

Pate guffawed. "Listen to yourself. Since when were you single, alone and having a baby?"

"You know what I meant. Taylor reminds me of my mom. That's all."

Pate shot him a knowing look. "Uh-huh. Sure. That's all. And sweet baby boy reminds you of you."

Wilder clamped his hands tighter on the steering wheel. Was that it? Was that why he couldn't stop thinking about Taylor? "Maybe."

"Well, why don't you just marry her and solve all her problems?"

Wilder's heart jumped. Ridiculous idea. Pate was losing it. "Why don't you just go back to sleep?"

Nevertheless, Pate's words lingered in Wilder's mind. He was a confirmed bachelor for good reason, and he'd stay that way. He wasn't about to take the chance that he'd end up a deadbeat dad or a cheating husband like his own father and brother. As the saying went, blood was thicker than water. Rob Gadsden might not claim him, but his blood flowed in Wilder's veins.

Besides, Taylor wouldn't want the likes of him. She'd loved Cale, probably still did, even if his brother had broken her heart. Cale had been the handsome charmer with money in his pockets and a wealthy family. Wilder was only a beat-up calf roper with little to offer but hope and a dream.

A dream he'd lose if he didn't stay focused on roping calves instead of on his pregnant housekeeper.

The ranch was too empty. Again.

Taylor called herself a fool for missing Wilder

Littlefield. No matter how nice he was or how much his childhood story touched her tender, hormonal emotions, he, like Cale, was a professional rodeo cowboy. He was off to Texas and who knew where else to chase the National Finals. Surrounded by admiring women and fans.

Hadn't she learned her lesson about rodeo cowboys?

Except Wilder was different.

She thought.

"Oooh." She was driving herself up the wall.

Taking a basket filled with a jar of goat milk and a small plastic container of herbed cheese she'd made herself, Taylor waddled down the front steps, rubbing Veronica's nubby head in passing.

Good old Veronica had proved herself useful in many ways. It was hard to believe Wilder wasn't fond of such a valuable creature.

There was Wilder again, back in her thoughts.

Aggravating.

She wished he was here this morning. He'd get a kick out of what she was about to do.

He could have snapped photos for her blog.

Once in the car, she drove a mile, parked on the road fifty yards from Flora's driveway and crept quietly up to the torn screen door.

With her puffy feet, there was no chance she could escape without being seen, but she wasn't worried. She and Wilder had left little gifts on Flora's porch three times now and escaped unscathed.

Esther never failed to produce a daily egg, which actually belonged to Flora.

Wilder might make treks to Flora's out of "love thy neighbor," but Taylor was in it for the adventure. She got a thrilling adrenaline rush every time. Not as good as zip-lining over the Grand Canyon but exhilarating, nonetheless.

Except it wasn't as much fun without Wilder to laugh with afterward.

Other than a squirrel chattering at her from the tree next to the house, Flora's property was quiet. To Taylor, Flora's home always felt abandoned. Which she found infinitely sad.

Placing the basket by the door, she knocked and hurried away as fast as she could.

Behind her, the door scraped open. Taylor's pulse jumped.

"Girl! Stop. What are you up to now?"

Caught red-handed, Taylor spun around.

In a faded, baggy green dress, Flora peered at her through the rusted screen.

"I thought you might like goat cheese and milk?" Taylor's words ended in a question. Her heart banged against her rib cage.

Instead of answering, Flora came out on the porch and glared at her. "What's wrong with your feet?"

Her feet? The old woman noticed her feet? "Too much salt, the doc says."

Flora motioned her to come closer, jabbing a

bony finger toward the porch steps. "Sit down. You got no business running around like this, jarring that baby, swelled up like the Goodyear Blimp."

Ouch. That hurt.

Taylor sat anyway, relieved to be off her feet for even a moment. The fifty-yard walk seemed longer today than usual.

So far, she'd seen no sign of the rifle, and Flora seemed inclined to talk.

As she propped her fat feet on the top step, a sigh escaped. Her legs throbbed.

The older woman stood above her, glaring down.

"You're seeing the doctor, you say?"

"Yes, ma'am. Over in Centerville. Dr. Burns."

"I wouldn't know him. Is he any good?" Again, the tone was so gruff, Taylor felt like a kid caught stealing candy.

"Dr. Burns is a woman. She seems to be good. Busy, but knowledgeable."

"Huh. Busy. They're all too busy these days. Well, don't you be missing any prenatal visits. Not with those feet." She stabbed a finger toward Taylor's snug flip-flops.

When had her ankles gotten so big?

"Yes, ma'am."

Again those sharp eyes pierced Taylor. The woman could poke a hole with those eyes. And that cranky voice. "How's your blood pressure?"

Taylor blinked a couple of times. Really? The

cranky neighbor wanted to know about her blood pressure? "Okay, I guess."

"You *guess*?" Flora hissed through her teeth. "Girl, you got to take responsibility for your own body. Get into town today and get yourself a blood pressure monitor. Pregnancy is a responsibility you shouldn't take lightly. That child depends on you."

Taylor cringed. "Yes, ma'am."

The doc had said nothing about her blood pressure.

"Where's that sneaking cowboy of yours anyway? I saw him pull out of here in that rig of his. You shouldn't be alone." Flora huffed. "Worthless men."

Taylor didn't bother to clear up the misunderstanding about her relationship with Wilder, but Flora's sharp-tongued parenting advice made her wonder.

"Do you have children, Miss Grimley?"

Flora stiffened. Some awful emotion—pain, grief, horror—distorted her face. Whirling away, she stomped inside the house and slammed the door behind her.

Later that day, Taylor drove to the Mercy Mercantile in search of a blood pressure monitor. Flora's sharp comments had made her nervous. The other woman's negative reaction to a simple question about children made her curious too.

What was that all about? Had the woman lost a child?

Milly didn't have a monitor in stock but offered to put one on order.

"Are you ailing, honey?" Milly asked. "Is everything all right with you and baby?"

"We're fine. I saw the doctor earlier this week. But my feet are swollen and Miss Grimley insisted I should get a monitor."

"Flora Grimley? Are we talking about the woman who speaks to no one unless to order them off her place with a shotgun? Even the UPS man leaves her packages at the end of the driveway."

"She's just a lonely old lady, Milly." She told her about the fun adventures she and Wilder had had, and that each time they'd come away unscathed. "We've noticed that she never comes out to chase us away until after we finish doing whatever good deed Wilder has thought up."

Milly laughed. "Y'all are sweet, you know that, and that Wilder—he's a dandy fine man—but you got to be careful." She pushed her glasses up on her nose. "There's a rumor about Flora I've heard ever since she moved into that old place years ago. As much as I hate to say it, hon, you shouldn't go around her. Leave her be."

"What kind of rumor?"

"I'm not one to spread tales, but seeing how you're in harm's way, I better tell you."

Milly glanced around the store, leaned across the counter and began to speak.

Chapter Nine

Wilder killed the engine, leaned on the steering wheel and stared at his house. Taylor had hung one of her pretty flowered wreaths on the front door. The blue door he'd grown to appreciate.

Fact of the matter, he appreciated all the other things she did around his property to keep it looking clean and occupied. Bright and cheerful. Before she'd invaded his space, he'd frequently come home to overgrown grass, an empty refrigerator and a house that looked abandoned.

But not anymore.

As much as he was looking forward to having his bedroom back, he was starting to dread the day she left. Where would she go? What would she do? She wanted to travel and write her blog, but her former blogs were all about adventure and thrills. How could she shoot rapids or explore caves with a baby in tow?

He sighed and stepped out of the truck.

Not his business.

Except it was in a way. Baby boy was his nephew, and he was starting to care about that.

He'd tried to talk to her about the future after

the baby's arrival, but she'd simply said, "We'll manage."

In other words, she didn't need his input. They were friends, trading housework for a temporary place to stay.

He placed a booted foot onto the bottom step of his own front porch and paused.

Was Taylor up yet? He didn't want to disturb her. She needed her rest.

The morning was early, barely sunrise. He'd driven straight home after two nights in Mesquite.

Pate had laughed at him for turning back toward Mercy, called him "Uncle Daddy" and had gone on to Amarillo with another cowboy.

Wilder didn't care. He'd wanted to come home. The weekend earnings had kept him in the game, though he still clung by his fingernails to the number fifteen spot. This upcoming weekend, he'd head to Fort Worth, only a few hours' drive down the same highway he'd just traveled. The payouts there were decent.

If he won.

He tried not to worry about that, but the number fifteen nagged at him like a gnat in the ear. Two other cowboys were hot on his tail and climbing fast. Hanging on to last place was risky, dangerous. He needed to move up in the standings if he wanted to secure that career dream of making it to the NFR.

Just once. That's all he asked. One trip to Vegas

to make a name for himself and Huck and ultimately the horses he'd raise and train to sell to other ropers. One trip to secure his future and the permanent home he'd always longed for.

Later today, he'd visit Jess's ranch for roping practice.

His belly growled. He patted it. Right now, he needed food.

Taking his phone from his back pocket, he texted Taylor. You up?

Her quick reply surprised him. Just now. How was last night's event?

A pleasant warmth filled his chest. Sweet that she would ask. Why don't you come outside and we'll talk about it.

What? What! You're home?

A half dozen exclamation points followed the entry.

I am.

In seconds the door flew open and a barefoot Taylor, in navy blue shorts and a stretchy yellow T-shirt, rushed down the steps and straight into his chest. She flung her arms around his neck and laughed.

He was so surprised, he backed off the step onto the grass and took her with him.

But he had to admit—holding Taylor in his arms felt really nice. Baby bump and all.

"I haven't had a greeting like that in—ever," he said, a chuckle rumbling from his chest.

Did that admission sound pathetic? He hoped not. But he didn't lie. Unless he counted Milly's back-from-the-dead embrace which was entirely different, Wilder had never been greeted with such enthusiasm. Jess shook his hand or slapped him on the shoulder when they met, but no one hugged him much since Mom passed.

Something seemed to lodge in his throat. He cleared it. "Glad to see you too."

To his deep regret, she leaned back a little. Not much, but he liked having her close. She smelled clean and fresh like spring flowers. Or those oils she put in her goat soap. Really nice.

She smiled at him with such sweetness, Wilder was tempted to kiss her. Her bow mouth tilted and her blue eyes were wide and sparkling. All it would take was a light tug and a head dip.

He waited. She didn't move away.

Time seemed to hold its breath. Or was that him?

Maybe because she seemed happy to see him, or maybe because no one ever greeted him with such enthusiasm, but he really wanted to kiss her.

Wilder leaned in, testing the waters, unsure if this was a good idea, but wishing it was.

It sounded good to him.

Her lips parted. She breathed a minty-fresh sigh.

"Wilder?" Her voice was soft, curious and sounded as puzzled as he felt.

"Yeah. It's me." Sliding his hands up the back of her soft hair, he pressed her closer.

This was madness. She was only his housekeeper. Except she was quickly becoming a lot more.

He lightly rubbed his thumbs along the side of her neck beneath her ears.

Taylor shivered. "That feels nice."

Her arms, looped over his shoulders, tightened, drew him near.

Just as he'd given up the battle and decided to kiss her, the baby moved. Kicked. Thrashed. Gut-punched him.

He froze.

The shock of her belly moving against him stunned him. The movement was a strong reminder of why he should not get personally involved with Taylor. This was Cale's baby, not his. She loved his brother, not him.

No use starting something he could never finish.

The slap of truth put an ache in his chest. He couldn't change what was…even if he wanted to.

Dropping his arms to his sides, he backed away.

Taylor watched the big cowboy's face turn from tender to troubled. A deep flush crested his sun-tanned cheeks.

"Sorry," he said.

Sorry? He was apologizing?

His reaction hurt. But she deserved it. What had she been thinking to throw herself into Wilder's arms as if they were more than friends?

She'd missed him. That's what she'd been thinking. She had so much to tell him that she'd been excited to have him home.

For the briefest moment, when she'd realized he'd driven all the way back to Three Nails Ranch when he'd planned to keep traveling, she'd thought he'd returned because of her and the baby.

Maybe he had, but not in the way she'd imagined.

Not because he was feeling anything more than concern for her and the little guy he claimed as nephew.

Her wildly excited reaction to seeing him on the front porch had shocked him. And her. She hadn't expected to like Wilder this much.

Wilder was a straight-arrow Christian. He probably considered her an immoral idiot, jumping from one man to another indiscriminately. She wasn't. She didn't.

The only man she'd ever thought she'd loved was Cale, and she'd fallen out of love with him at his funeral. Publicly learning that your husband, or the man you thought was your husband, was married to someone else, could do that.

She'd stood numbly, strangers looking on, while his wife and parents called her every evil name possible and demanded she leave. She'd felt dirty and used, and she never wanted to feel that way again.

"I got carried away," she said, a hot flush burning her face and neck. "Sorry too."

Shifting awkwardly, Wilder rubbed the back of his neck and allowed the tiny grin she'd grown to like so much. "It's okay. Getting a welcome home is a rare thing for me. As in never happened. I kind of liked it."

"Okay, good. I don't want things to be awkward between us again."

"If they were still awkward, I wouldn't be here."

"So why are you? You're supposed to be roaming all over Texas winning roping contests and climbing the PRCA standings."

"I am. I will be. Right now, I'm hungry." He patted his belly, a reminder that *her* belly had repulsed him. "Are the girls keeping pace?"

Appreciating his efforts to move on from the embarrassing moment, she answered, "The girls are stellar layers. Come in and make your own coffee while I rustle up some grub."

He opened the door for her and stood to one side. "Talking cowboy now, are you? Rustling up grub?"

She grinned and entered the house, relieved to be back on comfortable terms.

No more almost-kisses. No more over-the-top reactions that must have been caused by hormones.

No more thinking about Wilder every minute of the day. None.

No more.

She had a goal to reach, a travel blog to write and that meant traveling again ASAP. Her swollen feet itched to get moving. She was not a stay-in-one-place woman.

Accomplishing something she, and she alone, had done was the only way to prove to her family that she could and would be successful without their input.

Not that she was doing such a great job of it at the moment, but she would. As soon as baby arrived and she could pack up and move on.

She didn't want to fall in love ever again. Never.

Considering his repulsed reaction to the baby's movement, Wilder didn't want that either. In fact, the very first time she'd met him, he'd made it clear that he was not interested in love and marriage.

Like her, he'd been caught up in the moment.

She, the discarded mistress of his half brother, was the last person on earth Wilder would want.

The kitchen was complete chaos.

Wilder gazed around at the various pots, boxes, craft items and tiny bottles of good-smelling oils that lined the counter and the island.

Taylor took his klobase sausage from the freezer and whacked off a couple of slices. "Sorry about the messy house. I wasn't expecting you today."

"No problem." He scratched his ear. "But where's the coffee pot?"

She pointed toward a lower cabinet. "Cheryl came over to work on crafts last night and by the time she left, my legs couldn't take any more."

Cheryl Janicka. Like everyone else around Mercy, he knew the woman. She and husband Aaron were solid folks. He'd bought his share of fresh tomatoes from her garden and frequented Aaron's small engine repair shop. No one sharpened mower blades like Aaron.

He put the coffee on to brew and went to wash up. As he did, he recalled Taylor's words. Her legs were bothering her.

On return to the kitchen, Taylor had the eggs and meat sizzling in the pan. Wilder wanted to stare at her feet and legs but didn't. She might take it the wrong way.

So he waited until her back was turned.

He didn't know anything about pregnancy but her feet looked like water balloons.

Leaving the coffee pot, which didn't need his watchful eye, he went to her and took the spatula away. "Sit down."

"What?" She blinked at him.

"You said your legs were giving you trouble. Sit."

"I don't need a keeper."

"Agreed, but you need to get off those feet before they bust."

Her mouth opened, closed, opened again. She

looked down. Grimaced. Then pulled two chairs away from the table, sat in one and propped her feet on the other.

She studied them, poked a finger into one. "They're only this bad because I stood up too long last night. This tile floor does that. Makes my back hurt too."

"You should rest today, keep your feet elevated and take better care of yourself. Nothing here is that important."

She shot him an amused glance. "You sound like Flora Grimley."

He flipped the eggs with one hand and pushed down the toaster lever with the other.

"Flora? Since when are you having a conversation that doesn't begin and end with 'Get off my property'?"

Taylor told him about the odd encounter on Flora's porch. "She insisted I monitor my blood pressure and take better care of myself."

He shook a generous dose of pepper onto the eggs. "Flora Grimley said that?"

Taylor, in an imitation of Flora's gruff tone that made him chuckle, said, "Girl, you better take charge of your own health. That baby depends on you."

"I'm impressed. Five years of trying and I've never gotten a semikind word out of her."

"My guess is, she doesn't much like men. Especially Christian men, for some weird reason." Taylor leaned back and stretched as if trying to make more room for the baby. "But that's not the important part. Listen to this. It's pretty shocking. When I went to Milly's to order a monitor, she shared a rumor about Flora's past."

"Shocking how?" Wilder clicked off the stove, filled his plate with eggs, sausage and toast, and joined her at the table.

She handed him the ketchup and the hot sauce.

It was kind of nice to have someone know his preference for spicy eggs.

Even nicer to have a pleasant conversation with a smart, interesting woman while he ate breakfast.

As soon as the thought came, another floated by. This one was about cozy mornings and husbands and wives and the comfort of having someone special in his home for good.

He threw the ridiculous notion to the ground and tied it with a double hooey.

That kind of thing was not for him.

Scowling, he shook out an extra dose of Louisiana Hot Sauce, hoping the spice would burn the errant thoughts right out of him.

"Why are you frowning? I haven't told you yet," Taylor asked, oblivious to his thoughts.

"Was I?" Wilder forced an empty expression and shoveled in a forkful of fried egg.

"Yes, so brace yourself."

The hot sauce scalded the back of his throat. He

reached for his coffee, wishing it was ice-cold instead of fresh from the pot.

He sipped. Coughed. Grabbed for his napkin. His eyes watered.

Taylor dropped her swollen feet to the floor and started to rise.

Wilder waved her back down.

Taylor ignored him, filled a glass of water and placed it on the table next to him.

She sat again, watching him with concern and caution.

When he'd found his voice, he said, "Thanks. Too much hot sauce."

"You feeling okay now?"

"Feeling stupid. I know better."

She shuddered. "I don't know how you eat that anyway. I'd die of heartburn."

"My bad taste in food aside, what was it you were saying about Flora?" He added one extra cough and cleared his throat.

"Oh, yes. Right. Brace yourself."

"You said that already."

"It's worth saying twice. Seriously, I can hardly believe the rumor's true, but according to Milly, Flora has been in prison. She's an ex-con!"

Slowly, Wilder set the water glass on the table.

Temporarily forgetting about breakfast, he blinked at Taylor and tried to soak in this stunning revelation.

"What? Why?"

Taylor helped herself to his toast, tore off a corner and nibbled. "About thirty years ago, she was accused in the death of a new mother."

His mouth dropped open. He could barely wrap his head around this shocking information. "How? What happened?"

Taylor shrugged. "Milly didn't know. There are many different versions. Some say she was a doctor who tried to cover up a botched delivery. Others say she was a childless nurse, who wanted the woman's newborn for herself. Another rumor is that she was an unlicensed midwife, delivering babies in homes, and someone died. Anyway, she was some sort of health care worker who went to prison for homicide."

Wilder put his fork down. Blinked twice. "No."

"Yes. Sad, isn't it?"

"Sad? It's scary, Taylor. She's never hurt anyone around here, so I thought the shotgun was all bluster from a fearful old lady living alone. I never considered that she might be seriously dangerous."

As casual as if they were discussing goat's milk, Taylor lifted the hair off the back of her neck and twisted it into a knot on her head. He couldn't help noticing the smooth curve of her neck and how elegant she looked with her hair up. Like a ballerina.

Not that he'd know a thing about ballet dancers.

"Oh, Wilder," she said, patiently, as if he was a child. "Flora's not dangerous. She's just a sad, lonely, broken old lady."

For all her world travel, Taylor was naive. First Cale and now Flora. Definitely naive. Wilder liked to think the best of people but this news about Flora worried him. Not for himself. For Taylor. And the baby. She was alone out here.

What if Flora had insanely murdered a woman to steal her baby? Taylor could be in real jeopardy.

"You don't get sent to prison for no reason, Taylor."

"I know that, but if the rumor is true, she's paid for her crime."

Right. She had. He wanted to respect that and show Christ's love to his neighbor, and he would. But Taylor was the one who concerned him. Taylor and his nephew.

"Don't go over there anymore. Stay away from her."

"What?" Taylor's arms dropped to her sides. She sat up straighter. "What did you say?"

He should have been warned by the blue flames shooting out of Taylor's eyes that he'd just stepped in a pile of something regrettable. But he forged ahead anyway. "I think it's a bad idea for you to be around her. You're pregnant. Don't go over there again."

She shot out of the chair faster than he thought possible considering her bulk. "It is not your place, Mr. Littlefield, to tell me where I can go or who I can see."

The sweet voice he'd enjoyed a few minutes before was suddenly as hard and cold as a Minnesota pond in January.

Both palms raised, Wilder kept his tone conciliatory. "I'm just saying, it would be safer for me to look in on Flora. I'll drop off Esther's eggs or whatever. Let me do it for you. You steer clear. I'll handle everything."

For some reason, this kindly intended offer made his housekeeper even madder.

"Don't. Don't you dare!" She poked a finger at the air so hard, he thought she might break the sound barrier. "Do not *ever* presume that I need you or anyone else on this planet to take care of me. I am a perfectly capable adult."

Wilder stared at her for long moments, bumfuzzled, unsure of his next move. For a man whose career depended on fast thinking and quick reactions, he was frozen in the chute.

He was not a man who liked conflict, nor did he like having Taylor glare at him as if he was Jack the Ripper.

Lord, I could use some insight right about now.

He took a deep, still-burning breath and, as Jess had taught him to do, remained still, listening deep inside for a response to his simple prayer. God never shouted. If Wilder didn't listen close enough, he'd miss that holy whisper of direction.

As gently as the whisper inside him, he said, "Did I hit a hot button?"

"Yes." The answer was short, crisp. She was still fired-up.

He pushed away his plate, appetite as long gone as his paternal relationship. And probably as gone as his growing relationship with Taylor. His gut felt like he'd swallowed a brick. "I apologize."

"I make my own decisions," she insisted, not ready to let go. "No one runs my life."

"Understood." He hauled in another breath. Held it. There were so many things he wanted to say, questions he wanted to ask, but that small, still voice reined him in. "You're a strong woman, like my mother was. I admire that. Respect it. No one can doubt your ability to stand on your own two feet." Shooting for humor, he aimed an eyebrow at her feet. "Even if they are as puffy as marshmallows."

The stiff posture left her body. Something—relief, maybe—settled behind her eyes. "Thank you."

To further break the tension, he quipped, "Did we just have our first fight?"

Finally, the edges of her bow mouth quivered. "You don't fight."

"Not if I can help it." The poor kid in school with worn, secondhand clothes and no money for anything developed better ways to sidestep the taunting bullies.

"I admire that. Respect it." The tiny smile deepened as she imitated his words.

"Then, we're even?"

"Looks that way." She eased back onto the chair across from him.

"You're not mad at me anymore?"

"Never was." She rolled her eyes toward the ceiling. "Not much anyway. You're a hard man to stay mad at."

He emitted a short laugh. "I hope that's a good thing."

"I guess you're wondering why I'm adamant about making my own decisions."

"Maybe a little." A lot.

After a moment of thinking, she said, "Maybe someday I'll tell you."

Chapter Ten

Taylor figured she owed the cowboy an explanation for her over-the-top reaction. He'd been concerned, not trying to run her life, but for a second there she'd reacted as if he was one of her sisters.

He certainly was *not* anything like them. In fact, she'd never felt more appreciated or free than with Wilder. He accepted who she was and had never made a single rude comment, nor had he passed judgment on her for the colossal mistake with Cale. Quite the opposite. He'd been kindness and consideration personified, especially concerning her pregnancy and the child he'd easily claimed as his nephew.

What kind of man did that?

One as unique and unselfish as Wilder, apparently. Cale wouldn't have.

Even his Jesus-talk, which flowed out of him naturally, bothered her less all the time. Was his faith responsible for his kindness toward her? She thought so, and because of Wilder's example, she'd started rethinking her lost relationship with God.

Still, the questions about her parents' deaths remained. Why had God let them die? Why not her?

And why did she continue to carry this burden of guilt?

Sometimes she missed them so much she felt as if her chest would burst open. Times like now, when she was pregnant and scared much of the time.

Not that she would admit the scared part.

The idea of going home came, but, while going home meant security, it also meant giving up.

Surrender was not in her vocabulary. She'd rather be alone and scared than give up.

From beneath her eyelashes, she looked at the man sitting across from her.

She wasn't truly alone anymore. She had Wilder. And strangely enough, she was comfortable with him in a way she'd never been with anyone, not even her family. When he was home, she didn't feel so scared.

Wilder, the solid cowboy, who tried to do the right thing made her feel strong and smart and treasured.

Treasured? Where had that idea come from?

She turned the word over in her mind and realized that was exactly what she felt and the reason she could not stay angry with him.

Did he treasure *her*? Or just the baby she carried?

She wanted it to be both of them. And the unexpected desire troubled her more than her floundering blog income.

Before she could think better of it, she said, "I've been thinking about God lately."

As if he wasn't surprised, and he *had* to be, Wilder sipped his coffee and gazed at her quietly in that way of his that meant he was processing.

"He's thinking about you too."

The gentle response choked her up. She looked down at her hands, knotted in her lap, and swallowed.

"My parents died in a car wreck and…" She twisted her fingers so tightly, they cramped.

"And you blame God?" His husky tone seemed quietly understanding.

"Don't you blame Him for your mother's hard life? For her death? God is supposed to be in control, isn't He?"

"He is, but He lets us make our own choices."

That was the part that stabbed her in the heart every time. She'd chosen to do what she'd done. From the awful moment when she was eight to every single mistake since, the decisions had been of her making, not God's.

The guilt she'd carried her entire life foamed up inside like a shaken soda pop.

She wanted to rush into the bedroom, throw her things into a backpack and take off for parts unknown.

But she could never run far enough or fast enough to leave behind the truth.

Her heart pounded against her chest wall. She grew breathless.

Mom and Dad would still be dead.

"Which means—" her voice dropped to a whisper "—I killed my parents."

The disturbing declaration hovered in the kitchen for several long seconds like a wasp ready to sting. Outside, the goat tramped on the porch and bleated, probably eager to be milked.

Wilder ignored the sound. Taylor was hurting. Nothing else mattered right now, not his half-eaten breakfast or the fact that he needed to practice if he wanted to win this weekend.

His housekeeper was a complicated person. He'd known that from the beginning, but now he was beginning to wonder if she roamed the planet for her travel blog because she was running away from something more painful than the philandering father of her child.

"Impossible," he said. "You were just a little kid."

She glanced up at him. Her eyes glistened with unshed tears. "You don't know."

But she needed to talk about it. To him.

Wilder's chair scraped against tile as he scooted around to face her, knees to knees. He took her hands in his. Her fingers were cold and limp.

"You can tell me. I'm a pretty good listener."

"Will you hate me?"

"Not in a million years."

Her soft sigh touched a spot in the center of his rib cage.

"You won't tell anyone?"

"Well…" He drew out the word. "Maybe Huck. He's a good listener too."

The attempt at humor caused an almost-smile behind the teary eyes. "You tell your secrets to your horse?"

"All of them." He'd never had anyone, other than God, who he trusted that much. "So, go ahead. Tell me why an eight-year-old would think she was responsible for her parents' car accident."

"They were fighting." Taylor heaved a sigh. "Everyone thinks they had the perfect marriage but I know better."

"Even couples in a good marriage have an occasional disagreement."

She smirked. "How would you know?"

"Good question. But that's what my married friends tell me."

"Well, this was more than an argument over what color to paint the kitchen. They were talking about divorce. Mom was crying. They were both yelling. I was in the back seat with my hands over my ears, but they got louder and louder…"

Expression tragic, she put her hands to her ears as if she could still hear the ugly words.

The action just about did him in.

He wanted to hold her and make her pain go away.

"Have you ever told anyone else?" He started to

ask if her family knew, but she was touchy about their strained relationship.

"No. Never. Certainly not my sisters. Why hurt them with that knowledge?"

Wilder rubbed her cold hands between his palms. "Your parents' argument doesn't make you guilty of anything except being a silent witness."

"You don't understand. Mom leaned close to Dad, yelling, nearly in his face. He grabbed her wrist and pushed her away. Really angry and driving too fast in the rain. I was scared he would hit her. That they might hit each other." Taylor's voice cracked. "All I wanted was for them to stop fighting. Instead, I killed them both."

Wilder sucked in a shaky breath and waited. She couldn't be correct but somehow she believed she was.

Whatever had happened needed to come out before she could ever find peace of mind. "How?"

She swallowed, her elegant throat convulsing. "They were fighting so much that they didn't even notice when I unbuckled my seat belt. Or that I was crying hysterically. I begged them to stop. They paid no attention."

She shuddered and took several deep breaths before going on.

"I was afraid they would hurt each other. I had to stop them. So I leaned over the seat and grabbed Dad's arm. He jerked the wheel. We hit another car head-on." She closed her eyes, and when she opened them, it was as if she was reliving that horrible night. "I killed three people, Wilder. My parents and the driver of the other car. But I lived."

She began to sob. "Why did I live? Why me and not them?"

All Wilder's thoughts of keeping Taylor at arm's length went out the window. Holding on to her cold, cold hands, he rose, bringing them both to their feet, and pulled her against his aching heart.

If he felt more for Taylor Matheson than sympathy, he'd deal with it. Later.

Taylor wasn't one to wail and cry, but between Wilder's tenderness and the baby hormones, her emotions simmered, ever ready to boil over. Like now when she'd become a whimpering, sobbing bucket of grief.

Wilder must think she was a disaster.

Having his strong, calf-roper's arms around her felt better than anything she could remember in a long time.

Comforting. Caring.

Probably the same way he cared about Flora. Nothing romantic. Just another lost soul he was trying to save.

Right now she was okay with that.

His broad hand lightly rubbed the center of her back. Soaking in the consolation, she closed her eyes and rested against his thudding heart.

Rested. For indeed, she felt spent, as if telling him about the accident had emptied her.

Long moments passed while neither of them spoke and she wished she could remain cocooned this way forever, protected by Wilder's strength and surrounded by the scent of his aftershave and the sound of his quiet breathing.

When had Cale ever comforted her? When had he ever made her feel as important and worthy and cared for as she did with Wilder?

Never.

Yet, Wilder was only a friend offering refuge from her personal storm, a storm that had nothing to do with him.

No wonder her life was in shambles. She'd made more bad choices than good ones.

Wilder shifted, stroked a broad hand down the back of her hair.

His touch felt so good and right, she shivered.

"Were you hurt?" he murmured, voice rustier than usual.

Reluctant to tell him but knowing she would, Taylor nodded. Lying to Wilder was getting harder. "Some."

"How bad?"

"Bad enough. I was in the hospital and then in a rehab facility for several months."

Those were the days where she'd become a helpless, fragile invalid in the eyes of her sisters. From that day forward, they'd hovered, overprotected her, refused to let her grow up, until she'd finally left home to escape.

"Tell me." Again, those gentle, strong hands pressing against her back and hair encouraged her to speak.

"Crushed ribs, punctured lungs, broken pelvis, compound fractures of both arms and one leg." She recited the litany of injuries as if they'd happened to someone else, leaving out the fact that she'd been in a coma for three days.

Gently, he took her by the upper arms and eased her back from him.

Don't let go. Don't let go.

But of course, he must.

Kind brown eyes settled on her face. "That's horrific."

"I healed." She bit her lip, glanced away from his piercing gaze.

"Outside, but not inside."

Astute, insightful. How did she contend with a man who could see through her?

"Thank you for listening."

He cocked his head to one side. "Did it help?"

"Some."

Being held in his arms helped more than anything, but she didn't say that.

"You weren't responsible for the accident, Taylor. You're a very smart woman. Intellectually, you know that."

She sniffed, reached for a napkin on the table.

"In my head, yes, but in my conscience, no. If I hadn't intervened—"

"An accident likely would have happened anyway. They were arguing, distracted. He was driving too fast. Those things alone can cause an accident."

"I try to tell myself that, but I still feel guilty." She dabbed at her eyes and stuck the napkin in the back pocket of her shorts.

"Will you let me pray for you?"

His question should have been awkward. It wasn't. Not from Wilder, who seemed to talk to Jesus about everything as if they were friends.

Sometimes he reminded her so much of Poppy, the grandfather who'd prayed her back from the brink of death. Poppy too, prayed about everything. She even recalled a time when he'd prayed for a crippled cow and the very next day the cow was up and walking around.

Funny how she'd forgotten those things until now.

"I think I'd like that."

Standing close as a whisper, he took both her hands in his and began to pray. Not a pompous, fancy prayer but a quiet conversation with someone he knew well.

At first, Taylor kept her eyes open, observing the serenity in his face. Then, longing to know that same peace, she let her eyelids drop and absorbed his simple, heartfelt words.

Forgive me, Jesus, she inwardly prayed. *For-*

give me and help me forgive myself. I've been so angry, and I've made such a mess.

No bells rang. No choirs sang. But something light and peaceful expanded in her chest. Relief spread through her, a balm to her aching soul.

"I think God's not mad at me anymore," she blurted, interrupting Wilder's lovely prayer.

He shook his head, expression tender enough to make her teary. "He never was. The question is, are you still mad at Him?"

"No. No!" She tugged her hand loose and patted her chest. "I feel something amazing in here."

"That's Him. That's Jesus. You must have invited Him in."

"I guess I did," she said in awe.

Feeling new in the strangest way that she could never explain, she threw her arms around Wilder's neck for the second time that day. "Thank you. Thank you."

"Thank Jesus." He laughed lightly at her sudden change of mood. Holding her loosely at the waist, he pressed his forehead against hers. "I'm happy for you, Taylor."

And that's when it happened. The baby, cradled between them, once again moved.

A tiny gasp escaped Wilder. His gaze flew to hers.

"Was that…?"

Taylor nodded, suddenly tense. "Your nephew." She expected the cowboy to withdraw as he'd done before. Instead, he dropped his gaze to her middle.

"May I?"

She nodded, understanding, but surprised, realizing he asked to feel the baby's movements.

He laid a hand lightly on the mound that held his nephew. A broad, manly hand as rough and rugged as the outdoors touched her with such tender care, tears of joy, not of grief, sprang to her eyes.

The baby, as if recognizing his uncle's touch, stirred.

Wilder looked up, clearly awed. Their gazes connected.

"Amazing," he whispered. "Beautiful. Thank you."

Breathless with joy from Wilder's reaction, Taylor placed her hand over his and held it there while the baby performed his gymnastics routine.

Wilder was not repulsed. He was enamored.

Her heart gave one hard bump before Taylor caught herself.

Wilder was enamored of the baby. His next of kin. Not of her.

A significant difference.

But she, who'd vowed never again to let a man get close enough to hurt her, was in danger of becoming enamored of him.

Chapter Eleven

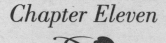

Wilder invited Taylor to go with him to roping practice. He wasn't sure she would agree, but after this morning, when she'd shared a secret with him that she'd never told anyone, he felt sorry for her and didn't want to leave her alone at the house.

That was it. Sympathy.

He had to admit, though, feeling the baby move had a strange effect on him. Suddenly, he felt possessive of the child as if the little man was his son. A fierce protectiveness rose inside him, a need to be a part of the boy's life, to be the man his father and the baby's father had refused to be.

If Taylor knew his thoughts, she'd accuse him of trying to control her life. She might even pack up and run. He didn't know why the idea bothered him. She'd leave at some point anyway. Travel was her goal, her dream, and she'd been very clear that no one was to interfere.

But he *was* the uncle. Kinship connected him to the baby. It also connected him to his father and half brother. Their DNA ran in his blood. The connection worried him, as it had since he was sixteen and vowed never to hurt others the way his mother—and he—had been hurt. That's why he was single, alone. Except he wasn't alone anymore.

He glanced at the woman in the truck seat next to him as they pulled onto Jess Beamer's Cross-Beam Ranch.

Taylor and her animals, her crafts, her laptop and her friends filled his ranch house.

Her presence was...nice. More than nice. It was special, like her. Taylor had given him someone to come home to after days on the road.

Don't get too attached. You know better.

But they were connected, would always be connected, by DNA, but also because of their experiences with the Gadsden men. She too, had been hurt by a Gadsden and now her son would be too. Just as Rod Gadsden had wounded him.

This afternoon, Taylor had changed into jeans and a long, stretchy T-shirt and pulled her dark hair up into a ponytail. He liked it that way. Her clear, smooth skin glowed and a double pair of small earrings flashed from her lobes. He wanted to stare at her fresh prettiness.

"Ever been to a roping?" He used the question as an excuse to look at her.

"Yes. My sisters were barrel racers."

This was one of the few times she'd mentioned her estranged family.

"Were you?"

"No." Her face closed up. She turned to stare out the side window, and when she didn't elaborate, Wilder realized he'd stepped in it again. Her family was off-limits.

As if intentionally changing the subject, which he figured she was, Taylor asked, "Is this the ranch where you always practice?"

His pickup rumbled beneath a crossbar and onto an idyllic ranch with pastureland spreading as far as the eye could see.

"This is the place."

She motioned toward the herd of horses peacefully grazing on thick, green grass. "Beautiful."

"Someday, I want Three Nails Ranch to look like this."

He'd spent three years with Jess on the Cross-Beam, learning to be a man, to ranch and raise horses. Here, he'd honed his roping skills with the former rodeo athlete. He loved this ranch and the people who'd taken him in when he had nowhere else to go. Without Jess Beamer, he didn't know what would have happened to him.

"You'll reach that goal, Wilder. I know you will. You're such a hard worker. This is your year."

Her compliment pleased him. She knew his goals of earning enough this year to retire from the constant travel. Interesting that he wanted to stop traveling and she couldn't wait to hit the road.

"I hope you're right. With Fort Worth coming up next weekend, I need to be in top form. A lot of good cowboys will be there."

"You didn't bring Huck. Is this where you keep your practice horses?"

"It is. I'll work Huck a little at home before I leave, but he's more juiced-up and ready if he hasn't run in a few days."

"I could take care of them for you."

He glanced her way. "My horses?"

"Sure. I'd love it."

So would he. "Better leave them here with Jess. You'll be leaving soon, remember?"

"Oh, right. Yeah." Some of the light left her expression.

Had he disappointed her? Made her feel inadequate the way her family did?

Wilder reached across the console and tapped her hand. "Thank you for offering. If you were here longer, I'd jump on the idea."

She gave a small half smile and turned toward the passenger window.

Tending her own animals was one thing. Offering to care for his felt personal. He liked the idea too much.

Wilder parked close to the corrals to save Taylor the long walk from Jess's ranch house to the barns in the back. Her swollen feet had to be uncomfortable.

"We need to get you some boots." He eyed the flip-flops she wore. Not exactly ranch attire.

She made a rueful face. "Wouldn't do any good until after baby arrives. I couldn't get them on."

He helped her out of the truck, grabbed a lawn chair from the back and offered an arm. Surprisingly, she didn't glare at him with terse reminders that she was perfectly capable of taking care of herself.

He knew that. Admired it. But he enjoyed helping her, touching her, being close to her. A man liked to be the hero even when the woman was as strong and capable as Taylor.

"Watch where you walk and look out for those naked toes."

She looped her hand around his elbow.

"You didn't have to bring the chair."

"What? You're going to sit on the metal fence or the ground?"

"I could."

"My nephew said no."

She flashed him an amused look. "Oh, he did, did he?"

"Yep. This morning. He tapped out Morse code. Being an expert, I got the message. He said to prop those feet up. With the chair, you can sit and prop them on the fence rail."

She bumped his side with her shoulder. "I can't decide if you're bossy, funny or nice."

He chuckled. "Let's go for the last two."

As they reached the barn, Jess Beamer came out to greet them. Though he'd passed sixty years old, the rancher remained fit with barely a paunch beneath his snap-front shirt, though gray fought with the brown in his short sideburns.

He clapped Wilder on the back and shook his hand. "I see you brought a friend."

"Taylor, this is Jess Beamer, best roper you'll ever meet and all-around good friend." He'd told her about the man who'd taken him in after Mom died. "Jess, this is Taylor."

Jess touched the brim of his hat. "Ma'am, it's a pleasure. Any friend of Wilder's is welcome on the Cross-Beam."

From the speculation in Jess's gaze, Wilder knew he had questions. After all, Wilder hadn't brought a woman to the Cross-Beam since he was seventeen and trying to impress Paige Wallace with his cowboy prowess. Now, here he was, not only with a woman, but a very pregnant woman.

A pregnant woman who was coming to mean more to him than was sensible.

"Got some calves ready for me?" he asked, eager to move past the topic of his housekeeper. He and Jess would talk but not now.

Later. Like dealing with his feelings for Taylor.

Jess motioned toward the barn. "Horse is ready. Mount up."

"Anything I can do to help?" Taylor fell into step with Wilder as he headed toward the silver metal barn. Jess circled around to the chutes on the other side of the corral. "It's been a while since I was around horses, but I'm a fast learner."

"I'd rather you rest. It's not that long until the baby comes."

He'd leaned the lawn chair against the railing but she wasn't ready to sit.

She patted her tummy. "Only a few weeks left, but doc says we're doing fine."

He looked down. "Except for the feet."

She playfully punched his upper arm. It was like a rock. "Stop with the feet, already."

He grinned. And Taylor realized how much she enjoyed having that grin aimed in her direction.

His rejection of her idea to bring the practice horses home to his ranch had bothered her at first, but he was right. She would be leaving soon. His refusal wasn't to cast doubt on her capabilities.

Inside the barn two horses stood, saddled and waiting, each with a boot-encased hind leg off the ground as they relaxed. Wilder ran his hands down the neck and hips of both animals before choosing the stocky bay mare.

Taylor followed his lead and stroked both animals. Their soft velvet muzzles and warm breath took her back in time. Harlow would let Taylor touch, sometimes even ride, an old deadbeat horse with no energy, but she was never allowed to race or work cattle.

She was her own boss now. She could ride like the wind if she wanted to.

"After the baby comes, I want to go riding."

Wilder stepped into the stirrup and tossed a leg over the saddle. He gazed down at her, expression serious and questioning. "We can do that. If you're still here."

"Right." Another reminder that she didn't belong here, with Wilder. Was he eager for her to leave?

She, an independent world traveler with plans and dreams and a blogging career to grow, was getting a little too content with a cowboy who had about as much interest in forever as a housefly.

And neither did she. Not after what Cale had done.

"You'll be okay while I rope?" He turned the horse to the side, still looking at her.

"Absolutely. Me and little man will behave ourselves and sit in the chair out by the fence."

His humor returned. He winked. "Prop up. An order from my nephew."

With a teasing glare, she waved him off and turned to exit the barn. She heard Wilder's tongue click as he and the horse plodded out to the chutes.

For the next two hours, she marveled at Wilder's speed and athleticism. For a man who moved quietly around the house, he was a fireball in the arena.

Over and over she watched in utter amazement and admiration as the chute gate clattered open, a steer shot out like a cannonball, and hot on his trail were an intense man and horse. Wilder already had the rope spinning over his head and let it fly, easily catching the calf. Every single time.

Dust flew beneath the horse's hooves as she skidded to a sudden stop. With a small rope called a piggin' string between his teeth, Wilder leaped from the animal's back, followed the now-taut rope, picked up the calf and laid him on the ground. He moved so quickly, Taylor gasped to see his hands in the air and the calf's legs tied.

With the horse holding the rope taut, Wilder returned to the saddle and waited the required six seconds before releasing the calf.

From the chute, Jess called, "Ten point one."

"Too slow." Wilder shook his head, disgusted, as he re-coiled his rope.

Taylor sipped the bottle of water she'd brought along and stared in disbelief. Too slow? She'd thought he was lightning fast.

"Looked good to me," she called, which caused Wilder to wave and smile.

"Are you getting tired?" he called back.

"I'm good." She extended her legs on the bottom railing and the horse blanket Wilder had draped over the metal to make her more comfortable. He was thoughtful that way.

Even though she was tired and dusty, she was enjoying herself. This was what Wilder did for a living. He was good at it. He worked hard, practiced hard and, as odd as it sounded, she was proud of him. As proud as if he was her man.

Every time he stopped by the fence to talk to her, Taylor's pulse sped up. She felt animated, attractive. As if she was important to him. And he to her.

Foolish thoughts. She should be embarrassed to develop a crush on anyone, considering her condition. Especially when that man had made it clear from the start that her time on the Three Nails Ranch was only a temporary responsibility he'd taken on out of the goodness of his heart. He was a Good Samaritan. That was all he was to her. Once the baby arrived and she was back on her feet, he'd expect her to leave.

And she would. That's what she wanted too.

Wasn't it?

She'd hugged him goodbye.

As Wilder traveled to Fort Worth and all throughout the weekend, his mind seemed stuck on Taylor, not on the work he had to do.

He'd thought he had his head together. He'd thought he was ready for the rodeo. He'd practiced every afternoon.

All with Taylor on the sidelines watching, cheering him on, making him feel big and strong and tough. And protective.

He'd never had a woman make him feel so much like a man.

Which was bizarre. He'd never even kissed her.

He sure wanted to.

When she'd tossed her arms around him and

hugged him goodbye, telling him to be safe and that she'd pray for him, he'd battled all kinds of emotions, including the ridiculous urge to kiss her and ask her to come along.

He hoped she didn't go over to Flora Grimley's place. He'd taken Esther's eggs and a jug of Veronica's milk to the woman as he pulled out this morning. Hopefully, that was enough to keep Taylor from engaging in a potentially dangerous activity.

Wilder rubbed a hand across his eyes. Yep. He should have brought her with him. Regardless of the curious stares and the inevitable uncomfortable questions, he'd worry less. She'd be safer with him.

If she knew his thoughts, she'd likely pack up and run far and fast.

A hand clapped him on the back. "Hey, Wilder, you're up next."

"Right. Thanks." He slapped his hat on his head, checked Huck's protective boots and adjusted his roping gear one last time before he mounted Huck.

Around him other cowboys with their mounts roamed the back of the chutes, preparing, talking or watching the action. The scents of hot dogs and popcorn mingled with horse sweat and leather.

Good smells. The smell of money.

He'd scored a 9.0 last night in his first go to put himself in third place. A good score tonight secured a decent paycheck and kept him in the running for the NFR.

Metal clanged against metal as a chute opened. A roar went up from the crowd. The voice on the PA system offered a play-by-play, praising the cowboy in the arena—Brant Cheatham, number sixteen in the standings, the man closest to Wilder.

"Ladies and gentlemen," the announcer bellowed. "Eight point three seconds for the Arizona cowboy."

Excellent score.

Wilder guided Huck into position next to the calf chute. He'd have to post better.

He and Huck could do it. They'd posted better before.

The crowd's excitement stirred Huck's competitive blood. He pranced in the box, eager. Wilder's adrenaline jacked. His pulse kicked up.

After a glance to see that the calf was in place inside the chute, he nodded, piggin' string between his teeth, rope already in motion.

He heard the clang of metal, saw the calf make his break. Huck, in a burst of speed, flew into the arena.

They were fast. Wilder felt it. This was it. He could move up tonight.

He let the rope fly…

…and missed.

The rope fell to the ground along with his hopes. The calf bucked and trotted out of the arena.

Wilder sat on his horse, too stunned to do anything except reel in the empty rope.

He hadn't missed a throw in months. He and Huck had been penalized for a broken barrier a time or two but they hadn't missed their calf.

Barely aware of the crowd's disappointed murmurs and the announcer's commiserations, he tugged his hat low and walked his horse out of the arena.

One more event remained. One more chance to improve his score. He'd need a big one if he hoped to stay in the race.

As he dismounted, cowboys, who cheered each other on no matter the competition, greeted him.

"Bad deal," someone said.

"Sorry, Wilder."

"You'll get 'em next time."

All he could do now was watch the rest of the competition or go back to his trailer.

From the back of the chutes, he watched for a while but his heart wasn't in it. He'd expected a big win tonight and he'd gotten nothing.

He propped a boot on the railing and immediately thought of Taylor with her swollen feet on Jess's metal fence.

Pulling out his cell phone, he scrolled to her picture. The one with the goggles, rubber gloves and crossed eyes.

Looking at her cheered him.

"Lord, keep her safe."

The cowboy standing next to him leaned in.

Dusty was new to the circuit, just a kid, but a nice guy. He was low in the standings but moving up.

"That your wife?"

Wilder's stomach lurched. "Housekeeper."

The kid whistled through his teeth. "Wish I had a housekeeper who looked like her."

Wilder chuckled. "Even with the goggles?"

"It's what's behind those goggles that's mighty pretty. Big blue eyes get me every time."

"Yeah," he conceded. "She's pretty."

She was also pregnant with his brother's child. He didn't say it but he needed to remember it.

He also needed to stop thinking and worrying about her and focus on this rodeo. Another bad night or two and he'd be watching the NFR on TV.

Maybe he should call her, make sure she was okay. Then, he could put her out of his mind and get on with the business of winning tomorrow's go-round.

Chapter Twelve

Taylor hung up the phone after nearly an hour of talking to Wilder. He'd tried to make light of the no-score event, but she could hear that he was down. She tried to cheer him with a funny story about Veronica and Esther, who'd become friends. The hen rode on the goat's back whenever Taylor let her out of the chicken pen. Veronica seemed to enjoy the company and waited at the gate until Esther, whose leg had healed well, could come out to play. It was the cutest mismatch.

Wilder, true to his nature, had laughed and suggested she blog about the unlikely friendship.

She loved the idea and planned to work on it this very night. Tomorrow, she'd take photos and hope her readers and sponsors weren't turned off by more down-on-the-farm news instead of exciting travel blogs.

In calls to and from her sisters, they'd both questioned the change but claimed to love her ideas. Fortunately, they hadn't seemed suspicious about her location. Though Harlow lived half the year in Florida with her pro athlete husband, Monroe still roamed the Kiamichi Mountains with her pack of rescued dogs, only now she did so with her fiancé, Nathan.

She was thrilled that Monroe had found true love with a good guy, according to every family member she talked to, but meeting Nathan would have to wait.

Still, tonight she was lonely for news from her hometown. She didn't know why. Perhaps it was the nesting mode she'd heard about that happened before a baby was born. She refused to let it be about her conflicted feelings for Wilder.

Scrolling through her contacts, she tapped the number for her close friend, Tansy Winchell. Tansy was older by a few years but somehow they'd clicked as kids and never looked back. Through all of Taylor's four-year travels, they'd maintained contact. Tansy was Taylor's source for real news from home.

Even though her friend lived in the same town as Taylor's sisters, the newspaper reporter had never betrayed Taylor's secrets. Including the big ones— her pseudo-marriage and subsequent pregnancy.

While waiting for the phone to connect, she wandered out to the back porch to the patio chairs. They were new. Purchased by Wilder after he discovered her sitting in the dark on an upturned feed bucket.

Summer nights were the best. The air cooled and the stars shone like glitter in an inky black sky. Since surrendering her life to Jesus, thanks to sweet Wilder, she especially enjoyed staring up at the galaxy and thinking about God on His throne, watching over her.

The phone line clicked in her ear.

"Hey, girl. What's up?" Tansy's chipper voice was muffled.

"What are you eating?" Taylor knew her friend's propensity for snacks, especially sweet rolls from the Bea Sweet Bakery.

Tansy's laughter, still muffled, filled the line. "Caught me. Sage Trudeau made the most delicious, glazed lemon muffins you have ever tasted. I'll bring you some if you like."

"I'd love that. As long as you promise not to tell anyone where you're going."

"Cross my heart. You know my lips are sealed, although I don't know why you don't just toughen up and tell your sisters to go fly a kite and let you live your life."

"It's complicated."

"You're a coward."

"Am not!"

"No, you're not, at least not about most things, but this has gotten ridiculous. Taylor, you're going to have a baby. Don't you think they'd want to know?"

Yes, they would, and they'd be all over Taylor like ticks on a coyote, sucking the life out of her.

"I didn't call to hear a lecture, Tansy. I can get that from my sisters."

Back aching, she stretched. Baby boy was active tonight. She wished Wilder was here to make funny remarks about the little one's gyrations. According to the cowboy, her boy was practicing to be a bronc rider. Or a dolphin at SeaWorld. He was good at making her laugh, especially when she was worried.

"I love you, friend," Tansy said. "I just want you to be happy."

"I am happy. Sort of. Mostly." She told her about Veronica and Esther and her concerns about the blog. "What if my blog dies? What if everything I've worked and traveled for disappears while I'm waiting to have this baby?"

"What if it doesn't? Or if it does, why not resurrect it into something else, like stories from the farm?"

"You sound like Wilder."

"Wilder again, huh? The good-guy rodeo cowboy. You sure talk about him a lot."

Did she? She certainly *thought* about him often. But if she did, wasn't that natural since she saw him more than anyone else?

"Don't get any ideas, Tansy. I'm his housekeeper, who happens to be pregnant with his half brother's baby. That little detail has to be a major turnoff to any man."

"But you like him. And he likes you."

"He's great. Funny. Warmhearted. Generous. Considerate. An all-around nice guy." She lifted one hand in the air as if Tansy could see her. "He sleeps in a camper while I live in his house. Who does that?"

"A pretty special cowboy, if you ask me."

Yes. Very special. So special her heart fluttered each time he walked through the door. She was still sorting out her feelings over *that* troubling complication. "I treasure his friendship."

And miss him every moment he's away.

Tansy made a rude sound. "Go ahead and lie to yourself. You like him and that's okay. It's even okay if you fall in love with him. After the fiasco with that other cowboy, you deserve real love from a real man."

Taylor massaged the top of her belly. Would she ever again believe she deserved good things? She might not, but her baby did. "What would you know about falling in love?"

"Enough not to let it happen."

"There you go, then. I'm not letting it happen. Wilder doesn't want any emotional entanglements, and I don't either. I'm a wanderer, a travel blogger. Wilder is a homebody at heart who wants nothing more than to retire and live on his ranch. We don't fit."

The admission made her uncomfortable. Or perhaps it was this chair.

"You've fit pretty well for the last month or two."

They had. Which didn't mean anything. She was desperate and he was kind. End of story.

Except it wasn't. The troubling emotions were

eating her alive. She needed to talk, and who better to tell than her best friend? Wasn't that why she'd called in the first place?

"Wilder called tonight. He calls every night. We talk a long time." And text. Dozens of texts. Nothing too personal. From him, mostly photos of the rodeo or a funny GIF. And the daily inquiry into her health. She sent pictures from her latest craft endeavor or set of decorative goat soaps.

"Interesting." Static came over the phone and Taylor suspected her friend was reaching for another muffin. For a junk-food, carb-eating addict, Tansy somehow managed to remain as slim as a pencil.

It was so not fair.

As she pinpointed the Big Dipper, Taylor heaved a long sigh. "What if I *do* like him too much, Tansy? Didn't I learn my lesson about cowboys from Cale? What's wrong with me?"

Tansy muffled something into the phone, and after a pause in which she must have finally swallowed, she said, "One mistake doesn't define you."

"Again, you sound like Wilder. He even prayed for me. Out loud. And he prays for the baby every day."

"Wow. That's big. Try again to convince me that he's not into you *and* that baby."

Day before yesterday flashed through Taylor's mind. Wilder at the front door, saying goodbye, and before she could stop herself, she stepped out on the porch and hugged him. Beneath her ear, his heart sped up. He'd tugged her close, his chin resting on her head with a soft sigh.

In the morning air, he was warm, his muscled chest and arms a study in controlled strength. She'd felt special. Treasured.

The memory lingered like the fragrance of the lilacs she'd planted next to the front porch.

"I almost kissed him before he left for Fort Worth." She spoke casually, one finger in the air tracing the handle of the Big Dipper, but her insides jittered with the implication.

Tansy's breath hitched. A pause and then, "I wonder how he would have felt if you had."

"I don't know. When we first met, he kept me at a distance. I thought he was judging me as some evil Jezebel who played on men's sympathies."

"But now?"

"Lately, he's different. We're different. We have fun together. He's even interested in my constant chatter about all things baby-related." Which had nothing to do with her and happened, no doubt, because he and baby boy were related.

"You've gotten to know each other, and he's learned that you are an awesome person."

"He's the awesome one."

"There you go, then. You're single. He's single. You are both too awesome for words. Go for it."

Taylor groaned and stared at the brightening Milky Way. "Haven't you heard a word I've said?

I can't. We can't. Considering my situation, he'd probably think I've lost my mind if I kissed him."

"You'll never know until you try?"

Out in the chicken pen, one of the hens fluttered. Another squawked. And then several.

Taylor stood and walked in that direction. Predators prowled around her chickens. She'd seen their footprints after a rain.

"Hold on. My chickens are upset about something."

"Where are you?"

"Backyard. The sky is gorgeous. You should go outside more."

The waning half-moon and healthy eyesight guided her across the backyard, her flip-flops slipping on the dew.

Country quiet was deep and tranquil like no other. She loved it here, an admission that surprised her.

"Be careful out there."

"I am." She knew how to shoot a rifle but didn't own one. Her baseball bat was under the bed, not that she'd ever needed it out here. Yet.

The memory of her first meeting with Wilder flashed in her head. She smiled. She'd threatened him with a cast-iron skillet.

Too bad she didn't have the skillet with her now.

The chickens clucked and fretted, voicing upset about something.

Opening the gate, she stepped into the pen and

moved cautiously toward the enclosure. Any predator that managed to breach the hen house would be small.

"Please don't let it be a snake."

"What?" Tansy's panicked shout hurt Taylor's ears. "A snake? What kind of snake? Run. Get out of there."

"My chickens are in danger. And I couldn't run if my life depended on it."

She hoped it didn't.

"I need a flashlight."

"Use your phone."

"Oh, right. Great idea." Why hadn't she thought of that?

She aimed the flashlight app and slowly opened the door. All six hens, the rooster and eight fluffy yellow chicks huddled on one side of the roost.

Taylor flashed the light toward the other end.

"What in the world?" She moved closer, still cautious, but less afraid. "Tansy, you aren't going to believe this."

"Is it a cobra?"

Taylor laughed. "Yes. Since they don't exist in the wild in America, I have decided to add cobras to my chicken house."

"Be serious. What is it?"

Taylor reached for the tiny animal. It mewed.

"A kitten." A scrawny, dirty, shivering kitten. "I have no idea how it came to be inside my chicken house, but she's tiny and scared."

"Oh…" Tansy's voice melted.

"She's also scaring my chickens."

"What will you do with her?"

"First, I'm getting her out of my hen house. Tomorrow I'll see if I can figure out where she came from and return her. Tonight she gets to sleep in a crate in the kitchen."

Would Wilder mind having an animal in the house?

Hopefully, the kitten didn't have fleas.

Taylor shrugged. Too bad if he did. This kitten needed rescue.

Collecting the critter in one hand, she held it close to her chest. The cat nestled in and began to purr.

Securing the chicken house and pen once more, Taylor headed back toward the house.

"Look, Tansy, I need to take care of this poor little thing. I'll let you go. One last thing before I do."

"What is it?"

The grass was slippery. Taylor picked her way carefully across the wet surface. "Baby boy is due in three weeks. Are you coming to the hospital to see me?"

"As much as I hate hospitals, I'll be there."

Taylor hated them too. They brought back terrible memories. "Bring muffins. And cinnamon rolls."

Tansy laughed. "You got it, pal. Will Wilder be there?"

Would he want to be? Did she want him to?

Deep down, she had to admit she did. Wilder was becoming way too important.

"I haven't asked, but he's serious about the uncle thing." The baby kitten squirmed, crawled up her shirtfront and began to nuzzle her neck.

"He's probably waiting for you to ask."

"Maybe. I don't know." If she asked, then what? Would he feel obligated? Would she?

Their relationship had taken a turn the day she'd told him about the car accident and they'd prayed together. She'd felt closer to him, as if they were a couple.

Scary, scary thought. He'd probably run backward if she told him. She wouldn't, not with all the conflicted feelings running around inside. Even her best friend didn't know the whole truth.

Maybe she didn't even know herself.

She'd already made too many mistakes. She wouldn't let Wilder be another.

After sleeping off a headache in his camper, Wilder awoke with a knot in his gut and a burning desire to go home, to breathe the clean country air and, if he was honest, to make sure Taylor was all right.

"I shouldn't," he told Huck, as he loaded the horse into the back of the trailer. "You want to run and I need to make more rodeos this month."

As if he sympathized, Huck nuzzled Wilder's

chest. Wilder rubbed the sides of the long face, his forehead pressed between Huck's soft eyes.

Around them, other cowboys loaded up, metal doors clanged, hooves pounded against wooden floors. Humidity thickened the air and lifted the smells of rodeo and diesel exhaust.

This had been his life for sixteen years. As much as he loved the sport, he was tired. Tired of the road mostly, but today he was both tired and discouraged.

Yesterday morning, he'd attended cowboy church in the arena. Something the preaching cowboy said stayed with him.

"We all want to win every go-round," the preacher said into the microphone, "but we won't. We know it. Apostle Paul knew it too. He talked a lot about sports and athletes, about how hard we work to win that elusive prize. Only one cowboy wins the big earthly prize. When we're not that top cowboy, and maybe we don't even earn back our entry fees, it hurts. None of us want that, but when it happens, and it will, we need to turn our focus to the eternal prize that all of us can gain."

"I press toward the goal to win the prize of God's heavenly calling in Christ," Wilder murmured to Huck, paraphrasing the Scripture passage. Just as quick, another paraphrase flowed into his thoughts. *Set your mind on things above.*

With a heavy sigh, he took the lead rope and guided Huck into the back of the trailer.

"I'm trying, Lord. I'm trying." Earthly things sure had a way of interfering.

As he secured Huck's back door and turned toward the truck cab, Pate approached.

"You going home?"

"Yup." Wilder waited for the inevitable teasing.

Instead, Pate offered a knowing grin. Not that he knew anything. He just thought he did. "Can a man hitch a ride?"

"Weren't you headed to New Mexico?" The same direction Wilder should go if he wanted to regain his lead. And then to Colorado and Wyoming where bigger money could be made.

Pate shrugged, but concern replaced his grin. "Shelby called this morning. Both boys are sick. She had to take off work again and the boss isn't happy. We can't lose her job."

Wilder heard what Pate didn't say. Shelby's paycheck kept them going when Pate's didn't. Plus, her job came with health insurance.

Rodeo wasn't for the weakhearted.

"Grab your stuff. We'll stop for breakfast later."

In a few minutes, they rumbled out of the bumpy parking lot and were on their way home.

Home. A real home since Taylor had taken over his house.

"What's wrong with your boys?" He pulled onto the highway leading through the Dallas metroplex and eventually to Mercy, Oklahoma. Traffic was moderate, a blessing in this city of shark drivers.

Pate kicked back in the passenger seat, boots stretched out before him. "Not sure. Shelby thinks they have strep. She's taking them to the doc as soon as I get home to watch the baby."

"Baby okay?"

"So far. Let's pray she doesn't get sick too. I hate it when one of my kids is sick. I'd rather be sick myself."

"You and Shelby are blessed to have each other to lean on."

"We are." He snickered. "She drives me up a wall sometimes but I'm wild about her. She's a great wife, terrific mother. I'd jump in front of a train for that woman." Squirming in the seat, he repositioned and propped his boots on the dash, ankles crossed. "A man needs a wife, Wilder. You ought to get one. They're great."

Before Wilder could think of an adequate reply, Pate pulled his hat over his eyes and slumped low.

Sometimes Wilder envied his married friends, but he didn't need a wife and kids to juggle with his career. It wouldn't be fair to them, would it? Or to him. Pate's situation this morning proved that.

But he was concerned about Taylor's future. Who would she lean on if her baby became ill? Who would help her, calm her fears, encourage her the way Pate and Shelby did for each other?

Over the next few miles he ruminated on the problem while Pate snored. When he spotted a

Chick-fil-A sign, he tapped Pate's shoulder. "How about a chicken sandwich?"

Pate mumbled something Wilder considered agreement, so he exited the four-lane into a business district flanked with fast-food restaurants and a strip mall.

They parked and went inside to eat and gulp cups of coffee. When they'd finished, they each ordered a giant lemonade to go.

As they walked back into the sunshine, Pate pointed his paper cup toward the strip mall. "Mind if we go over there for a minute?"

"A baby store?" Wilder sipped his tart lemonade.

"A kid store too. Shelby likes this place. I'll be the hero if I take the kids a toy to cheer them up."

Pate was a good dad, buying toys for his kids, loving them through their illnesses.

Wilder had never had that.

Taylor's son wouldn't either.

He took a giant sip of lemonade, swallowed hard and followed Pate to the store.

Chapter Thirteen

Holding the bathed and defleaed kitten in her hands, Taylor talked to Flora Grimley through the woman's ripped screen door.

"What is that you've got?" Flora sounded as grumpy and angry as ever. "A cat?"

Taylor held the mewing animal closer to the screen. "I found her. I'm looking for her owner."

"You won't find one. Heartless people dump kittens all the time. Whole litters of them. She's probably feral."

"She's not feral. She's very sweet and gentle."

"Well, let me see her." Flora shoved the screen door open. "Bring her in."

Taylor balked. She'd never been inside Flora's home. Wilder's warning came back to her loud and strong. Flora was an ex-con, convicted of killing a woman who'd just given birth.

Had the death been intentional? Accidental? What had happened?

But she wouldn't ask.

She also wouldn't go inside the house. She could if she wanted to. Wilder was not her boss. Someday she'd go inside.

But not today.

"I really don't have time, Miss Grimley. I'm canvassing all the neighbors." A sum total of four houses in a three-mile section. She'd already phoned the Mercy Mercantile and asked Walt to put up a sign on the store's bulletin board.

The sharp intelligence behind Flora's faded eyes saw right through the excuse.

Her face, open and interested before, closed up along with the opened screen door.

"All right. Go on, then. If you can't get rid of her, bring her back here."

Taylor could hardly believe her ears. "You'd take her?"

Flora's nostrils flared. "Don't go thinking I need a pet to keep me company. Mice are a problem out here."

"I understand." Probably more than the woman realized. Behind the cantankerous attitude, Taylor now saw what Wilder saw—a wounded soul, lonely but fearful of being hurt again.

She should have accepted the invitation to go inside. It was the neighborly thing to do.

The wooden door scraped shut with a curt snap, effectively cutting off further communication and any chance of entering the house.

Carrying the kitten close, Taylor continued her rounds, came up empty and headed back to the Three Nails Ranch.

As she neared the house, her pulse sped up. Wilder's rig was parked in the driveway.

She squinted.

What was he unloading from the back of his truck?

After parking behind him, she exited her Toyota and, with kitten in tow, hurried as fast as her bulk would allow to greet him.

Thrilled to see him again so soon, she walked into Wilder's arms for a hug.

If he was surprised, he didn't show it. Instead, he patted her back and made a pleased sound.

Tansy's words rolled through her head. What would he do if she kissed him hello?

She raised her head and looked into the rugged face that had become so dear to her.

His brown eyes, soft as a baby blanket, sparkled. "Guess what I bought?"

"What?"

He stepped back, creating an immediate vacuum, mostly in her heart. "Come in the house and I'll show you."

At that moment, he spotted the kitten nestled in the crease above her belly.

"You got a kitten?"

"Found her in the chicken pen." Struggling with emotions she didn't want, she waited while he tugged two shopping bags out of his truck cab. "She's a sweetheart. I call her Hummer because she purrs all the time."

His soft eyes went from the cat to her. "You've

collected a lot of critters. What will you do with her when you leave?"

Those troubling emotions threatened to boil over. "I probably won't keep her. Flora wants her."

Scowling, he paused at the front door to unlock it. "You've been to Flora's house again?"

She pointed at him. "Don't start."

But in reality, she liked his protectiveness. Not that she'd let him boss her around, but being with a man who cared about her well-being felt good right now.

With a head shake, Wilder sighed, shuffled the bags and let her go inside first.

Another nicety she'd miss when this interlude, or whatever it was, ended. Wilder was unerringly courteous, even with his hands full of shopping bags.

"What is this?" She put the kitten on the floor and stared at the giant box in the living room.

The cowboy shifted on his boots, grinning, his tanned cheeks dark with a flush and his eyes shining with eagerness.

What was going on?

"I brought something for the little man. Go on. Open it. There's more in the back of my truck." Before she could move, he produced a pocketknife and proceeded to cut the packing tape.

Then he stood back and waited for her to look inside.

"Wilder." Moved, stunned, she breathed the word. "What have you done?"

"It's a bassinet."

"I see that."

"A baby can't sleep on the couch."

"I've been thinking about that." She'd vacillated between preparing a room for him or preparing to leave as soon as he was born. The latter held less and less enticement as the days passed. She blamed fatigue and the nesting instinct, figuring they'd both go away after the delivery.

Would they?

"I don't know what to say."

"You don't like it?" His expression fell. "I've overstepped. Too pushy?"

Slowly, she shook her head, her heart filled to the brim. The gesture, the thought, the time and money he'd put into such a gift, touched her to the soul.

Emotion bubbled up like lava, warm and gushy.

Silly hormones.

"Hey. Don't cry. I'll take it back."

Was she crying? She touched her cheeks. "No, no. That's not the problem. There *is* no problem. I'm not mad or sad. Oh, Wilder, this is the sweetest. I'm touched and overwhelmed and—oh!"

Tiptoeing up, she kissed his cheek. "You. You."

His disappointment turned to relief and then to pleasure. "You like it."

"Yes. And I like *you* even more. You are the most thoughtful, kindhearted, generous—"

Before she could release a dozen other complimentary adjectives, Wilder stopped her…with a kiss.

A surprised gasp escaped her, but since she'd been wondering and Tansy had planted ideas in her head, she did what she'd done for the past four years. She lived in the moment.

Wilder's kisses, which went from one to several, at least one of them initiated by her, were exactly like him. Warm, strong and genuine.

Time seemed to stand still. For all she cared, she'd remain here in this man's arms all day. All month. All year.

Safe. Admired. Treasured.

There were movements and noises on the periphery but all that mattered in that segment of time was this moment with Wilder.

Taylor heard the kitten sharpen her claws on the strewn packing material. Wilder's phone went off a few times and then abruptly stopped as if the other party realized they were interrupting something important. They were.

Her heart beat in her chest and rose into her throat, ticking like a clock's second hand. Wilder's warm breath against her face. His hands on her cheeks, kissing her as if he'd been thirsty for a long time.

She'd been thirsty too. Not for kisses per se, but for what he gave her that no one else had. Respect.

When the kissing stopped, he didn't let go of her,

either with his hands or his eyes. A gentle smile curved his mouth. Oh, that wonderful mouth.

"Wow," he said, as bemused as she. "I need to buy more baby furniture."

Her own lips curved in response. She touched his jaw. He hadn't shaved this morning and his whiskers prickled against her fingertips.

Concern replaced the tenderness in Wilder's gaze. He scraped a hand across his chin. "Did my beard scratch you?"

"I never even noticed." She stepped back to regain her composure.

For she was most decidedly discomposed.

In her travels she'd had her share of kisses. None had meant quite as much as these, and she needed to reflect and understand why.

Was she, as Tansy suspected, falling in love with Wilder Littlefield?

She couldn't. Could she? Falling in love meant giving up her plans and letting someone else control her life again.

She was not about to let that happen.

Stepping away from temptation, for Wilder's sweetness was a huge temptation, Taylor motioned toward the giant box.

"Want to help me set this up?"

Wilder noticed Taylor's sudden withdrawal, the way she averted her eyes and focused on his gift.

Was she sorry he'd kissed her? That she'd kissed him too?

He wasn't. Not one bit, though he could practically hear Pate laughing in his ear.

He cared for Taylor. More than a little—and these unexpected emotions scared him to death.

The bassinet was easy to put together. Wilder tossed the instructions aside and spread the pieces across the living room floor. She'd polished the wood flooring again, he noticed, and the kitten slid spread-eagle as she leaped and jumped at every wiggling piece of plastic and paper.

The cat was a good distraction, as was the bassinet.

He might be building a baby bed, but he was thinking about Taylor and those unexpected kisses. Maybe some men went around kissing women without attaching any importance to it or to them, but he was not that guy.

So what was going on?

"You have to read directions, Wilder." Taylor collected the sheet he'd tossed aside.

"Nah. It's self-explanatory."

When she began to read the page aloud, he laughed, already completing the first step before she finished reading about it.

Taylor, who'd somehow lowered her pregnant self to her knees next to him, stopped reading and playfully whacked his arm with the instruction sheet. "Smarty-pants. I can do this myself."

"I know you can. But I want to."

She shrugged. "Go for it, big guy. Where will we put it?"

He found the other casters and snapped one into a supporting leg.

"We can clean out the extra bedroom I use for storage. Since it's across the hall from your room, he'll be close by."

He still didn't understand why she wouldn't use his main suite with the nice bathroom, but she adamantly refused. She claimed it was too personal now that she knew him, which he didn't quite understand. "The walls are already a light blue. Perfect for a boy's nursery."

"Your exercise equipment is in there."

"There's room in the barn for my stuff." He inserted a bolt into one of the legs and felt around the floor for the screwdriver.

She handed him the tool. "You've thought this through, haven't you?"

"Yup. My nephew needs his own room." He frowned at the unassembled parts, remembering that she'd leave. Even if she'd kissed him as if she wanted to stay. "At least while he's here."

Was he reading too much into a few friendly kisses?

"I could keep him in with me. Some mothers do that, but others say I won't get any rest if I do." She worried the corner of one fingernail. "I've never been a mother before, so I don't know what's best."

Wilder sat back on his heels and considered. Taylor carried a load far heavier than a baby. Alone, without caring family, she had no advisor that he knew of. She had friends, talked to them on the phone and told him about them, but right now, she needed family.

He wasn't much but he was here, and even though he wasn't *her* family, he was family to that baby boy.

"Tell you what. The bassinet is portable. We'll set up the nursery, and if you change your mind, we'll move him in with you. Deal?"

A look of relief turned to a smile. He sure liked to see her smile, would do about anything to watch that bow mouth curve.

"And," he added, to make her smile again, "if he cries too much, he can bunk with me in the camper."

As he'd intended, she laughed. He watched her, saw the way her nose crinkled up and her eyes shone like stars. She was beautiful.

He didn't want her to leave.

Which meant he was in serious trouble.

Later, after the bassinet was in place along with the tiny chest of drawers and all his rarely used exercise equipment moved to the barn, Wilder went to Jess Beamer's ranch to rope some calves. He invited Taylor to go along but this time she refused, eager to fuss with the baby's room.

He had to admit he was pleased by her thrilled reaction, though the kiss that had turned to something stunning, troubled him. He'd loved kissing her. Loved that she kissed him back.

That was what worried him.

He roped a dozen calves and missed four before Jess left the chute and walked around to where Wilder and his practice mare waited.

"Got something on your mind today, son?"

Wilder's chest filled with the endearing term. No other man had ever called him son.

"I guess I do."

"I thought so. You never miss this many calves. Trouble?"

"Maybe."

"Want to talk about it?"

"No, but I need to." Stomach tied in more knots than a roped calf, he dismounted. "I've prayed about it, but I'm coming up short of answers."

"Okay. Let's grab a glass of tea."

After tending to the mare, Wilder followed Jess into the long, traditionally styled ranch house. When he'd first moved in with Jess, after his mom died, Jess's wife was still alive. Abbie had welcomed him with open arms and a big heart. Though the couple never had children, Abbie was a teacher, and she and Jess claimed and mentored many children. He was one of them, the only one they'd taken into their home.

He missed Abbie's warm presence. He couldn't imagine how hard life without her must be for Jess.

The kitchen was clean and neat, not even a dish in the sink.

"Place looks good."

"Housekeeper was here this morning."

After Abbie died, he and Jess had done a decent job of keeping things clean, but with Wilder grown and moved to his own place, Jess hadn't wanted to bother. So he hired a weekly cleaning lady.

"Which brings me to my problem."

"You need a housekeeper? I thought Taylor handled that for you."

"She does. She's the problem."

"Ah." Jess nodded. "I wondered."

Wilder took two glasses from the oak cabinet and filled them with ice from the front of the modern fridge.

Jess, tea pitcher at the ready, poured the drinks, and the two men wandered to the table where, as Jess liked to joke, "They'd solved all the problems of the world at least twice."

Chairs scraped against old-fashioned terra-cotta tile as they settled in.

"I don't know where to begin."

"Begin with Taylor. She's messed up your well-ordered world."

Wilder huffed a short laugh. "You got that right. I missed my calf at the rodeo last weekend in round two. I never miss. Then, I didn't do so hot on the other two. If I don't pick up pace, I may lose my shot at the NFR."

"Why aren't you on the road to the next event?"

"I keep coming back home even though I know I should keep traveling. I can't seem to help myself."

"I see." Jess's sun-spoked eyes narrowed in thought. His was an interesting face, bronzed and shaped from mixed Choctaw ancestry and years of outdoor living.

"Taylor's pregnant, Jess."

One corner of the older man's mouth twitched. "I kind of guessed that."

They both chuckled at the obvious.

Lifting his glass, Jess wiped condensation from the tabletop beneath it with his shirt sleeve, though his focus was on Wilder. That was the way with Jess Beamer. When you talked, he listened hard and heard a lot more than Wilder ever said. He listened with his heart.

"You've kept quiet about her for the most part. What's her story, if you don't mind my asking? How did she end up living in your house?"

Wilder filled him in on the basics, including her heartbreak with his half brother. "Her job, her dream, is to be a successful travel blogger. Her blog is great, that's not the problem. She's witty and talented, makes you want to visit every place she's been."

"So what is the problem?" Jess swigged his cold tea and set the glass down again.

"What will she do with a baby when she's hiking Mount Everest or jumping out of an airplane over a volcano or some other crazy adventure?"

Jess blinked in disbelief. "She's going to do those things?"

"Not that exactly. But she'll be on the move all the time, going from place to place to gain fodder for her blog. A kid needs stability."

One eyebrow lifted as Jess narrowed in on the real issue. "A kid who happens to be your nephew? Right?"

"Yeah. Yeah. That. He matters to me, Jess. I want a good life for him."

"And you think his mother can't give him what he needs?"

"Not that at all. She'll be a great mom, but—" Insides whirling with unrest, he couldn't quite explain what he meant.

"I think I hear what you're not saying, Wilder. You and your mother moved a lot, didn't you?"

"We had to. You know that. When Mom couldn't pay the rent, which was often, we moved on to someplace cheaper." Even if cheaper lodging meant their rusty old car.

Sometimes they left in the middle of the night and his mom would send a few dollars a month until she'd repaid the outstanding balance. She always paid, although the extra effort of integrity added to her poverty. And his.

"Moving around like that was awful," he admitted. Life in general had been tough. He didn't want that for any kid, much less his blood kin.

"So, you're worried your nephew will experience the same heartache."

"Absolutely." His throat tightened.

"Valid point." Jess nodded and leaned in closer, one elbow perched atop the table. "What do you propose to do about it?"

"I don't know." Wilder pushed the half-empty tea glass aside, troubled. "Taylor's been pretty clear that she does not want to settle down and she sure doesn't want anyone else telling her how to live her life. Gets her riled up."

"Hmm. Interesting that she'd say those things. I've watched the two of you together. What I see and what you're saying are two different things. What's going on?"

This morning flooded back with the power of a monsoon. He'd kissed Taylor like a love-starved maniac. Bought her baby stuff. Hurried home to see her.

"Nothing. Well, something, but it can't happen."

"That's the crux of the matter, then. You want to care for her and the baby but she's not on board."

"Yeah, yeah, I guess that's the issue." Except Taylor was sending out all kinds of mixed messages. "She and I want different things out of life."

"You're in love with her?"

Wilder reached for his tea glass to gulp down

a thick wad of confusion. "Maybe. I'm afraid I might be."

Jess chuckled, dark eyes twinkling. "Love is a good thing, Wilder, not something to be afraid of. I wouldn't trade one minute I had with Abbie for anything except Jesus."

Seeing the nostalgia, the sense of loss in his mentor's eyes, Wilder said, "You and Abbie had something special."

Jess tapped the table with one finger. "I want you to have that too, son. A love for the good times, the bad ones and everything in between. A woman who appreciates the man you are, and you put her on that pedestal all women deserve."

Wilder sat back, shook his head. "I can't. Not with my history."

"What history? Your mother was a fine woman doing the best she could."

She was, but the memory of her hard life never left him for a minute. He would not do that to Taylor or any other woman.

"I meant my other parent, the absent, philandering, self-centered jerk who refused to take care of her."

Jess's wise eyes registered understanding. "And you."

"Yes. And me. His blood runs in my veins, whether I like it or not."

"Meaning?"

"What if I'm like him? What if Taylor and I did

fall in love, and I fail her the way my half brother failed her? He inherited our dad's ways. Maybe I did too."

Jess laughed. The man had the audacity to laugh at Wilder's struggle.

Wilder crossed his arms over his chest. "It's not funny."

The older cowboy instantly sobered. "More tea?"

Wilder pushed his glass toward the pitcher. "Thanks. I'll get the ice."

He got up and got more ice for both of them.

When he was reseated, Jess said, "I apologize for laughing. It's not funny, but it is ludicrous for you to believe that you are somehow anything like those other two men."

"DNA—"

"—is not all there is to a man's character. Your biological father didn't raise you. Your heavenly Father, with help from your sweet mother, instilled you with the character of a good man. The fact that you worry about treating someone badly says you won't."

"I don't know." But he wanted to believe.

"Listen to me, son. According to God's design in Genesis, man and woman were created to be together, a partnership of love and unity that should last forever."

"I know the Scriptures, Jess."

"But have you thought about what the opposite means? A life alone, as I am now? It's not healthy.

Single people die sooner than married, did you know that?"

Wilder laughed. "Trying to scare me into marriage?"

"Trying to talk some sense into you. If you care for Taylor, man up and talk to her."

He had, hadn't he?

And her responses had been as clear as polished glass.

Except for those kisses, which had muddled the scene tremendously.

Chapter Fourteen

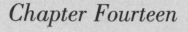

By the weekend, Pate's boys had mostly recovered from strep throat, and he and Wilder were both eager to enter the rodeo in Oklahoma City. The payout was good and a win there would go a long way to secure his position. Best of all, the four-hour trip wasn't a bad haul, though he needed to move on to the state fairs after that.

He wanted to keep an eye on Taylor and the baby too.

After talking to Jess, his head and thoughts had been clearer, probably because they'd prayed together before he'd left.

Today, as Wilder mowed Flora's lawn in the early dawn, preparing to leave for OKC that afternoon, his head had once again become muddled.

He figured if he delivered eggs and goat milk, mowed the lawn and otherwise looked after the cranky neighbor, maybe Taylor would avoid her.

She probably wouldn't. She felt sorry for the woman and blithely believed nothing bad would ever happen.

While he'd been gone to Jess's to practice, Taylor had even given Flora the kitten and made a trip into Mercy to buy all the supplies a kitten could possibly need. Including a scratching post, although, according to Taylor, Flora grumbled, saying she wanted the cat to catch mice, not be a lazy lap pet.

Taylor had loved telling him the story, especially the part about the kitten snuggling against Flora's neck and the way the old lady had melted like ice on a hot day.

He'd kept his mouth shut about the unnecessary trip, though knowing she'd gone to Flora's house again caused him more worry about leaving her alone.

Worry. When Scripture said to cast his cares on Jesus and let the Lord carry them.

"Easier said than done, Lord."

As he mowed, the engine drowning out his words, he talked to God, pouring out his concerns and confusion.

God was not the author of confusion any more than worry. The enemy was. So both worry and confusion were an attack against his peace of mind, sure as sunrise.

As he finished the dry grass and drove his mower out of her yard, aware that he'd likely not need to mow again this summer, Flora came out on the porch and shook her fist at him.

He laughed and waved.

"Wait 'til I tell Taylor," he muttered. Because Flora held the kitten against her shoulder, stroking its back.

Sure enough, Taylor, working at her laptop on

the kitchen table, stopped to clap her hands with joy. "I knew it. Just wait and see. She's softening toward us. That kitten is our breakthrough."

"You're an evangelistic soul and don't even know it."

"I'm learning from the best. Love thy neighbor as thy self."

How could he argue? She was repeating his oft-spoken words, and she looked so smugly cute, he had nothing negative to say. "Just don't endanger yourself being neighborly."

"Your laundry is done." Which meant she was changing the subject on him. She was like that sometimes. If she didn't want to deal with an issue, she moved on to something else.

"I told you not to bother with my stuff. I'll do it."

Taylor gave him that look. "You're not my boss."

"Technically, I am."

"Don't get smart." She turned back to the laptop.

He laughed, leaving her to her blog, which he would read tonight after the rodeo. Afterward, he'd have a reason to telephone her. They'd talk about the blog post, about his event and everything else they could think of. Sometimes the conversations went on for two hours or more.

Jess was right. He was falling hard for Taylor Matheson, the travel-blogging house sitter, whose laughter and wit, friendship and kisses lingered in his head no matter where he was.

He'd missed at least three events this week that

he'd planned to attend. Because of Taylor. And his nephew.

He was almost afraid to check the standings.

Two hours later, as he waited in Pate's driveway for the cowboy to kiss his wife and baby goodbye, Wilder opened his phone and finally looked at the latest calf-roper rankings.

His heart tumbled to the toes of his boots and died a painful death.

Sixteen. He was no longer on his way to the NFR. Unless he could earn considerable points and money this weekend, his dream was as gone as Taylor would be in a few weeks.

Both thoughts gave him indigestion.

Taylor sat on the back porch in the morning sun and responded to comments on her blog. Last night, she'd been restless with the discomfort of late pregnancy, and when the sun rose, so did she.

Now, as she waited for the hens to lay their treasures, she frowned at the limited responses to her latest blog post. Readers weren't as engaged as before. She'd also lost another sponsor, although, thanks to the soap-making posts, an essential oils company had shown some interest in signing on. Maybe she'd write more of those posts.

People also responded well to the two tales of Veronica and Esther. Considering that they were a constant source of entertainment to her, perhaps she'd embellish their antics and write more about the hen and the goat.

Pondering, she sipped the red raspberry tea recommended by Flora. Yes, she'd gone over there again the morning after Wilder had left. He wouldn't be happy if he knew. This time she'd taken freshly baked banana bread and invited herself inside.

There was nothing sinister about Flora's simple, tidy home. They'd shared bread, played with Hummer, the kitten, and discussed Taylor's imminent delivery. Flora insisted she try the red raspberry leaf tea in an effort to reduce the swelling in her feet and modulate her blood pressure, which tended to rise and fall at will, according to the monitor she'd ordered from Milly. After a quick internet search to be sure the drink was safe, Taylor had bought the tea and was giving it a try.

Something about Flora's sharp-eyed comments concerning her pregnancy made Taylor edgy, probably because of the ugly rumor. She wanted to ask the woman about her past but didn't have the nerve. She, who'd once swum with sharks, had become a coward. But she liked to think she was too kind to broach what might be a painful topic. Love thy neighbor and all that.

Feet propped on a lawn chair, Taylor took another sip of the fruity tea and then lifted her face to the sun to pray for Wilder and the day ahead. During one of their nightly phone calls, he'd confided that he'd fallen in the standings. Though he pretended the tumble didn't bother him, she heard the worry in his voice. He needed to win this weekend.

Although he'd made no such accusation, Taylor knew she and baby were to blame, and she felt guilty. Wilder had worked for years to get to this point in his roping career. She didn't want to steal his dream.

Rowdy, the rooster, crowed for the sixth time that morning, and one of the hens announced a safe egg delivery.

Which brought her back to her own delivery. Placing a hand on her belly, she stretched, miserable in her skin. She'd be glad when the day finally arrived. Her back ached. Fatigue and restless sleep had become the new norm. And oh, these fat feet!

Veronica ambled over, the bell on her collar jingling, to nuzzle Taylor and hope for a treat.

The goat was worse than a dog about begging for goodies.

Aimlessly running a hand over the knobby head, Taylor noticed dust rising on the gravel road. In spite of her self-talk to the contrary, her heart leaped. Was it Wilder?

One hand to her back, she levered herself up and walked around to the front of the house, hope bouncing inside with more activity than her son.

An unfamiliar Mercedes SUV turned off the dusty gravel road and into Wilder's driveway.

Taylor frowned, trying to place the luxury vehicle.

The doors opened and two well-dressed people stepped out of the car. An electric shock of adrenaline slammed into Taylor. Her every instinct screamed run. Run back inside Wilder's house and bolt the door.

Vivian and Rob Gadsden. Cale's parents. What were they doing here? After the awful things they'd said to her the day of Cale's funeral, she'd never expected to hear from them again. And had never wanted to either.

This could not be good.

Taylor stiffened her back and remained planted like a tree on the front lawn. She was stronger now. She'd faced them before on *their* turf. She could certainly face them on her own. Well, on Wilder's, but if he was here he'd stand strong beside her.

She wished he was here.

"Taylor, my dear girl." Cale's mother stretched out both hands as if greeting a long-lost friend. The sugary smile on her surgically youthful face instantly roused Taylor's suspicions.

Taylor shrank back, keeping her hands at her sides.

Why was Vivian, who'd called her every ugly name, behaving as if they were bosom buddies?

Vivian's expression hardened. Her smile disappeared.

"Taylor Matheson." Cale's father and, she thought

with a shock, Wilder's too, dispensed with niceties. Mouth flatlined and eyes hard, he came toward her with a sense of purpose, as if he was in a hurry and needed to make short work of an unpleasant errand.

Dressed like the attorney he was in shirt, tie and expensive slacks, he carried himself with the same arrogance she'd witnessed at Cale's funeral. Cale had been the same.

The lawyer's gaze dropped to her midsection. "It's true, then. You're pregnant."

Instinctively, Taylor's hands went to her belly. Her pulse accelerated.

Vivian must have noticed the protective action. She gave her husband a mild look. "Now, Rob, remember what you told me. We'll catch more flies with honey than vinegar."

Catch more flies? What was she talking about?

The Gadsdens obviously had not driven all this distance to apologize, but they wanted something and it wasn't flies. But what was it?

Taylor's pulse drummed against her collarbone. Anxiety rose in her throat. Her breath shortened.

"Why have you come here?" *And how did you find me*, although she'd worry about that later. "You were very clear at Cale's funeral that I have no part in your family."

"That was before we heard you were pregnant with our son's child." Vivian schooled her well-preserved features but her words cut as sharply as the blue eyes boring into Taylor's midsection. "His wife is devastated, as you can imagine, for more than one reason."

Taylor blanched. Cale's wife. The real one. "So was I. I'm sorry for her loss and yours. Cale, his lies and cheating, and his death hurt all of us."

The truth about their son didn't sit well with either Gadsden. Rob's tan darkened but he kept quiet.

Vivian, on the other hand, lost all pretense. Her claws came out.

"Do not blame my son for your mistakes. *You* hurt all of us. How could you show up at his funeral, flaunting your illicit relationship in front of his grieving parents and widow? Only the worst kind of woman would do such a thing."

Heat spread over Taylor's neck and cheeks. Humiliation, embarrassment but anger too. This woman had no right to seek her out for more vitriolic attacks.

Trembling, she said, "You need to leave."

"Now, Taylor," Rob said, his tone cajoling, "you'll understand that emotions ran high the day of Cale's funeral. We'd lost a son. Our hearts were shattered. Perhaps hurtful things were said."

"Perhaps?" She didn't even want to go there. "My heart was shattered too, but that didn't seem to matter. I trusted your son. I thought I was his wife."

Vivian sucked in a gasp. "Cale was a fine son and faithful husband until you came along and put your hooks in him."

Rob put a hand on her arm. "Vivian, please. I'll

repeat your words to me. Be civil. Let's work this out without too much rancor."

"Work out what?" Confusion and not a little fear rolled through Taylor. Her knees began to shake. Veronica, the goat, had followed her around the house, and now nudged her arm as if she felt Taylor's tension. "State your business and leave. Please."

Rob gestured toward the front door, the blue one that Wilder teased her about but admitted he liked. *Oh, Wilder. Come home. Right now.* She, who'd insisted on independence, who thought she needed no one, needed Wilder Littlefield.

"Let's step inside and sit down to talk, shall we? You look tired." This from Rob. "Perhaps we could share some refreshments, relax, catch up and discuss the most important matter at hand. Cale's child."

Cale's child? Foreboding crawled over Taylor's neckline like a black widow spider. She certainly would not allow them inside Wilder's home.

"There is nothing to discuss. I want you to leave."

The lawyer's mouth tightened. "That isn't true. The child you carry is our son's only heir. We are the baby's grandparents and as such, have a right to be involved in his life."

Fear tightened a grip on Taylor's stomach. "You do not. This is my baby and mine alone."

"Are you denying that this is Cale's child? We

have it on good authority from our private investigator."

Taylor's hackles rose. They'd had her investigated? Of all the low-down…"Whether he is or isn't is none of your business."

The lawyer in Cale's father didn't even blink. Quick as a rabbit, he switched to attack. "How will you take care of a baby?"

"I work. Again, none of your business." Taylor crossed her arms atop her belly, shivering, though the morning was already warm.

"You write a travel blog, which I cannot imagine generates any income at the moment and probably limited income at best. How will you provide for an infant? For a growing child who needs to be in school? For his medical needs or eventually his college?"

He shot the words at her like bullets, as if she was a hostile witness in a courtroom.

His questions were legitimate concerns that nagged her but he didn't need to know. She'd figure out a way. She always did. She had friends. Family if she grew desperate enough.

"Single women raise children on their own all the time. We'll manage." But she remembered Wilder's painful childhood and how he and his mother had struggled. She didn't want that for her son.

"Vivian and I can do better by Cale's child than simply 'managing.' We can give him everything and help make your life better too. With your co-operation, financial arrangements can be made, even a monthly sum, if you prefer."

Taylor's mouth dropped. She closed it, mind racing. "Are you offering me money?"

"Be reasonable, my dear. You're obviously in a bad situation now, which will only get worse after Cale's child is born."

Taylor clenched her teeth. She wished he'd stop saying *Cale's child.* "How can you possibly know my situation?"

"I make it my business to know things. Now, then. Let's behave like reasonable adults and get down to business." He reached out as if to pat her arm. She backed away. His mouth tightened, but he wouldn't rest until he'd presented his case. "We all make mistakes in this world. Cale made his. You made yours. Perhaps we were too hard on you at the funeral."

"You were. I was the innocent party, as aggrieved as anyone."

He dipped his head as if agreeing, though Taylor knew he did not. "You carry the heir to everything that would have been Cale's had he lived."

"I want nothing from you."

"Let's not be hasty. Let's look at the facts and see if we can come to a mutually beneficial arrangement."

She didn't even want these people for her son's grandparents. If they couldn't accept Wilder or her, they weren't the kind of people she wanted in her son's life.

"I'm happy the way I am. I don't need your 'beneficial arrangement.'"

He extended a hand, stop-sign style. "For your benefit and the baby's, hear me out. You desire to travel the world, writing your stories. That will be difficult with a child in tow. We are stable and mature, but still grieving and lonely, if you will. You're obviously a talented woman with your whole life ahead of you. With the right amount of financing, you can go on with your life as you were enjoying before this unpleasantness. We want your dreams to come true too, and we can make them happen."

His voice had become tender, kind, fatherly, far too nice. Like Cale, he was a good actor, able to manipulate others to his way of thinking. He must be dangerous in a courtroom.

After Cale's subterfuge, she knew to be wary.

No one who'd cursed her one day could suddenly have her best interest at heart the next.

"Mr. Gadsden, I have things to do. Will you get to the point and leave me alone? What exactly are you trying to say?"

As if she was a difficult child he was reasoning with, Rob closed his eyes momentarily and sighed.

"Here is the situation in plain language. You're giving birth to our son's only child, the child we need in our lives to help us heal from the horrible loss of *our* only son. Let's help each other, shall we? You need money to travel. We are willing to pay you a substantial amount to grant us custody of Cale's child when he is born." He named an enormous sum. "Even that is negotiable. We need Cale's child in our lives. Money is no object for us, but I daresay it is for you."

Taylor sucked in half the air in the Kiamichi Mountains. Shocked. Furious. Scared. She'd known they were up to something, but this was beyond ridiculous.

"I can't believe you'd ask such a thing. I don't want your money. While I am sympathetic to your heartache, I can't help you. This is my baby and he will remain *my* baby. He is not for sale." She turned toward the front door, her knees quaking. "This conversation is over."

Soft as a snake hiss, Rob's voice slithered down her back. "I am an attorney. A very successful one. I rarely lose in court."

His words stopped her in her tracks. She turned back around, eyes narrowed. "Are you threatening me?"

"Merely extending a kindly intended offer that I hope you will consider very carefully."

"I won't."

Taking a business card from his shirt pocket, Cale's father came toward her, hand extended. Though she wanted to run, Taylor took the linen card with shaky fingers. His handsome, tanned face was red and his eyes, she saw, were brown like Wilder's. In them she saw the pain of losing Cale and fought the sympathy that gathered beneath her breastbone.

The sympathy won.

Softly, she said, "You have another son, Mr. Gadsden, besides Cale. Wilder's a wonderful man."

A sob burst from Vivian.

Rob stepped back to put his arm around his wife's shoulders. "Regardless of what he may have told you, that rodeo bum is not my son. I have never been unfaithful to my wife."

Taylor would have laughed in his face if she hadn't been so upset. "Cale would probably have said the same thing. Which could be true, in my case. Maybe he wasn't unfaithful with me. I've never said this baby was Cale's."

"But it is."

Taylor simply gazed at him without words. If he didn't know for sure, perhaps he'd leave her alone.

Vivian leaned on her husband's shoulder, weeping. He looked uncomfortable with the emotional display but kept his eyes on Taylor.

"You've upset my wife. Again. If you have any mercy, you'll use that phone number."

He had a way of making her feel guilty when she'd done nothing wrong.

"I won't."

His nostrils flared. "Then, we will see you in court."

Chapter Fifteen

Wilder found the front door to his house unlocked and, after a quick knock, stepped inside. Taylor was nowhere in sight.

He set a large shopping bag on the nearby sofa and called, "Taylor?"

Her Toyota was out front, parked at a slant next to the house. Maybe she was outside with the animals. She loved sitting on the patio with Veronica and Esther while she worked on her blog or the next craft or researched a new kitchen science experiment. He loved that she loved it.

He was also concerned about her. She was closing in on her delivery date and he didn't like leaving her alone. She claimed she had friends who'd come when she called, but he still felt responsible. Maybe because he wanted to be.

He'd never thought about being a father, given his own father's rejection, but lately, especially after the conversation with Jess, being the baby's dad rattled in his head and heart all the time.

The past weekend events had been good to him and, even though he remained at number sixteen, he'd placed in all three rounds, so he was holding steady.

A quick trip home to check on Taylor and baby boy would clear his head so he could focus on the upcoming fair in Wichita Falls. The payout was big, and if he won there, he had a chance to move up again.

He could do it. As long as Taylor and son were okay. On the phone, she'd said she was, but he knew her well now. She'd downplay any problems and accuse him of trying to run her life.

Smiling a little at her sassy, independent streak, he was halfway across the kitchen to the back patio doors when a noise stopped him. He cocked his head, listening. Was that crying?

Slowly he removed his Stetson. The soft hiccupping sound came again.

Tossing the hat toward the island, he followed the sound down the guest hall and into the newly named nursery.

Taylor stood over the white bassinet, face buried in a soft, blue baby blanket, weeping as if her heart had broken into a million pieces.

His insides dipped, clenched. His mouth went dry.

Automatically, Wilder's gaze went to her middle. Was something wrong with the baby? With her? A dozen worries, the same ones that haunted him at night when he was away, sailed through his head.

"Taylor?"

She looked up. Her eyes were as puffy and swollen as her feet. And much redder. She'd been crying for some time.

He wanted to kick himself. He should have been here. If he hadn't stopped to eat and buy baby presents, he would have been home two hours ago.

Gently, he slid an arm around her shoulders. "Hey. What's wrong?"

As if a dam burst, Taylor fell against him, sobbing. Not knowing what else to do, Wilder wrapped both arms around her and let her cry. She clutched the baby blanket, soft as a horse's nose, against his neck, her fingers kneading the fabric.

After a while that seemed forever to Wilder, the sobs turned to sniffles. Wilder continued to rub her back and murmur idiotic phrases like, "I'm here. I've got you. It's okay. Everything's all right," when he had no idea if that was true or not. He didn't even know what was wrong.

Finally, she lifted her head but didn't move away. He was glad about that. She needed him and he loved being needed, especially by her.

Heart swelling, he gazed tenderly into her tearstained face and brushed away the brown hair stuck to her cheeks. "What's happened?"

Taylor shuddered in a breath. Tears welled again. And the fear in Wilder's throat nearly choked him.

He couldn't bear for something to happen to her. Or to his nephew. He loved them both. A fact he'd keep to himself. Taylor was a butterfly, flitting from place to place to make the world more beautiful. He had no right expecting her to land in one spot.

"Come on. You need to sit down." For once, she didn't argue or snap that he was not her boss. Docilely, she let him lead her to the rocking chair that had recently appeared in the room.

She sat and he knelt in front of her, taking her hands into his. "Are you okay?"

When she nodded yes, Wilder's bones went limp with relief.

"The baby too?" *Please Lord, let the baby be well.*

Again she nodded and Wilder could breathe again.

"Something's upset you. What is it?" His mind went a thousand places but couldn't land on anything that would upset her enough that she'd sob with such anguish.

He chafed her soft hands between his, gaze not leaving her face. "You can tell me," he prodded. "Anything. I'm here. Whatever you need."

He heard the desperation in his own voice for, indeed, he was desperate to fix whatever trouble she faced.

She shuddered in another long, shaky breath. Her body trembled until he could hardly bear it.

Finally, she whispered, "Cale's parents came here."

Shock ricocheted through Wilder like a bullet.

Cale's parents, which meant his natural father, had been on his ranch. And they'd upset Taylor.

Grimly, he said, "Not to see me, I'm guessing."

"I'm sorry, no." She wiggled one hand from his and touched his cheek. He leaned into the sweet gesture. Did she know how much her compassion meant to him and that even now, his father's refusal to claim him slashed a giant wound across his soul?

"What were they doing here? What do they want?" And why did his insides churn with longing mixed with anger and disappointment?

"They want my baby."

Wilder sat back on his boot heels. The shock of knowing Rob Gadsden had set foot on his property was nothing compared to this. "They what!"

Nodding, she covered her belly with both hands. "They feel they have a right to Cale's child."

"Your child." *My child*, he wanted to shout, but knew better. He was not the one she'd wanted. His brother was.

"Agreed, but they don't see it that way. They offered me money to give them custody. Money. As if my son was a toy they could purchase." She shuddered in a breath and pressed her eyelids with her fingertips. "Rob is a lawyer. I'm afraid he'll fight me and win."

"He won't. He can't."

"He said he'd see me in court. I tried to make him believe Cale wasn't the baby's father, but before they drove away, he said he'd force a paternity test."

Her shoulders began to shake. Tears tumbled down her cheeks. She fought them and failed.

Like his mother, Taylor was strong. If she cried, there was a very good reason.

A memory flashed through his head. He'd come in from school to find his mother sitting on their ragged couch sobbing into her hands. When she'd realized he was home, she'd put on a fake smile and claimed to have stubbed her toe on a chair. He hadn't believed her, but he'd gone along with the ruse to please her.

Later, Wilder had learned the reason. She'd lost the best job she'd ever had because she had refused the boss's advances. The same boss who owned their rental house thought he had a right to come over and spend the night.

Broke, jobless and homeless, they'd lived in their car that fall.

His mother had had no one to lean on. Taylor may not have a supportive family but she had him. He wouldn't let her face this alone.

"What if they take my son? I can't stand to lose him, Wilder. I love him. He's all I have."

The baby wasn't all she had. She had him.

Anger tightened his chest.

Wilder would fight the devil in his own territory to keep anyone from hurting Taylor.

He, a peaceful man who tried his best to emulate

Christ, wanted to pound his fist into something. Preferably Rob Gadsden's arrogant, selfish face.

"He had no business threatening you." Using the arm of the rocker as leverage, Wilder pushed off the floor and paced to the bassinet and back.

The anger refused to dissipate. He had to calm himself. He needed to think.

After a stern inner talk, he returned to the woman who'd been hurt by the same man who'd broken his own heart. And his mother's.

"I won't let anyone take your baby, Taylor. No matter what I have to do, he stays with you." *With us.* "You can trust me on that."

"What can you do to stop him? Rob Gadsden is a powerful lawyer."

"Maybe. But he's not God. The Bible says that no weapon formed against us will prosper and that all things will work to our good if we love God."

She slashed a hand across her cheeks. "I do. More all the time, thanks to you."

Wilder smiled tenderly at the woman who didn't know she owned his heart. "I was only the messenger."

Calmer now, and even more determined, he went to his boot toes in front of her again.

As he gazed into her tearstained face, his promise of protection rolling through him like a fierce river, an idea popped into his head. He liked this idea a lot but wasn't sure how she'd feel about it.

"I want to ask you something. I've thought of a

solution that could work. If you agree." Heart setting up a wild drumbeat, Wilder took her hands and held them against his chest. He wanted her to feel his sincerity. "Hear me out. Okay?"

Her gazed searched his, the blue, red-rimmed eyes tearing him apart. He had to make this right for her.

"Okay." Her fingers curled into his, giving him courage.

He wanted to speak lots of flowery words, proclaim everlasting love and devotion, but all he dared promise her now was that he would fight his birth father with everything in him so that Taylor would never have to worry about losing her son.

With a quick inhale, before he lost his nerve, Wilder blurted, "Marry me."

Taylor's first reaction to Wilder's unexpected proposal was shock, followed by a leap of pure joy.

And a gush of love so powerful tears welled in her eyes, though these were shed in happiness.

She loved this incredibly honorable man in a way she hadn't known existed. The emotion had sneaked in over time, building up with slow, steady tenderness with each moment spent in this cowboy's company until she knew, without a doubt, that she was truly in love. What she'd thought was love with Cale had been a whirlwind of infatuation and wild passion, as fleeting as autumn leaves.

Wilder was the steadfast kind of love.

But because she loved him, she couldn't accept his generous offer.

Wilder Littlefield had never wanted a wife. He'd told her so the first night he'd discovered her ensconced in his ranch house. Oh, he cared about her as a good friend, and he loved his unborn nephew. That was obvious by the gifts that kept appearing in the nursery.

But his offer of marriage was out of kindness, the very type of thing Wilder Littlefield would do. He was a giver, a love-thy-neighbor-as-thyself kind of man who would sacrifice himself and his dreams for a friend and for love of his nephew.

Pity, however, was no reason to get married. If she ever accepted another proposal, it would be forever and for the right reasons with a man who loved her unconditionally. Not because a kind, honorable man felt sorry for her.

Slowly, she withdrew her hands from his thudding chest and gathered the strength to do what she must.

"Wilder, you are the best man I know. I'm grateful for your kindness, but I can't marry you. It wouldn't be right."

The rugged face that moments before had been filled with hope, crumpled. He glanced to one side. His Adam's apple rose and fell. "I understand."

Did he? She hoped he did. A part of her was tempted to take the offer, anything to protect her son, but she knew that marriage to Wilder would not stop Rob Gadsden.

"You've been more than good to me, and I care for you." *A lot more than I'll say.* "But I can't let you do this. Even if I agreed, the Gadsdens won't back off. A paternity test would prove you're the uncle, not the father."

With a resigned nod, Wilder put hands to his knees and rose to his feet. Those strong roper's hands that moments before had tenderly held hers, erased the thought from the space between them. "Just an idea. Forget about it. We'll think of something else."

"And pray?"

His grin, though lopsided, appeared. "Absolutely."

But his eyes registered disappointment, and Taylor couldn't help wondering if her refusal had somehow hurt his feelings.

Rejection stung like a nest of mad hornets. Worse than losing an event or missing a calf with his rope. Every bit as bad as his father's cruel rejection all those years ago.

He understood. He really did. As she had reminded him, Taylor was having Cale's baby, not his. She was still in love with Cale's memory, not him. He was only a small-time rodeo bum with nothing to offer but himself and a remote ranch.

Taylor had no desire to be stuck in the middle of nowhere with a boring man like him.

No matter what Jess said, Taylor was itching to travel again, and she'd leave this one-horse town as soon as she could.

Still, some needy part of him had held out hope that she'd say yes, and he'd have the rest of forever to convince her to love him. Not his brother. *Him.* The illegitimate son, the castoff, who'd never been good enough to be a Gadsden.

Foolish on his part. He'd spent his life secretly trying to be somebody, striving to rise to the top of his profession in hopes of impressing one man.

One man who'd rather take away Taylor's baby than claim his only living son.

The ache in his soul grew hot and searing.

Giving his head a slow shake to clear the cobwebs, he made up his mind. Marriage or not, he was in this for the long haul. Or as long as Taylor stayed.

He felt a soft hand against his back and turned to find her standing a heartbeat away. "Are you okay? Did I hurt your feelings?"

Wilder's chest filled with love. She worried about him? When she was the one under attack?

"I'm fine. This isn't about me." Wilder pushed her hair behind one ear for an excuse to touch her. Her skin was soft beneath his rough, weathered fingertips.

Taylor moved closer and placed a hand against

his jaw. Her belly brushed his, a reminder of what was at stake. "Thank you for your kindness. I'm sorry I was such a crybaby."

"You're not. You're strong and smart. Together, we will figure this out." The baby moved against him. Innocent, precious, helpless and fully dependent upon the adults in his life to protect him. Wilder was determined not to let him down. "As long as I have breath in my body, this baby remains where he belongs, with you."

Chapter Sixteen

Her weekly doctor's visit seemed useless to Taylor. All the ob-gyn did was measure her belly and proclaim the baby was now at thirty-seven and a half weeks' gestation. She already knew that.

Still, a thrill ran beneath her skin to know that in a couple of weeks, she'd hold her son in her arms.

As she drove home from Centerville, she stopped in Mercy to mail three autumn wreaths and to deliver a batch of lavender soap to the Mercantile. Her crafts were selling well both there and online. Even though her travel blog continued to flounder, she'd picked up readers and orders to augment her income.

She wasn't getting rich the way she'd hoped when she'd begun this adventure four years ago, but the money kept her afloat until she could travel again.

Taylor gnawed the corner of one fingernail.

Travel concerned her more all the time and not only because she'd be traveling with a baby. She worried that the Gadsdens would use her vagabond ways as a reason to gain custody of her son.

Wilder despaired too. She could tell. Even

though he bravely declared he wouldn't let it happen, how could he stop the legal system?

Staring through the windshield at the tiny town that had embraced her like a friend, Taylor suffered an unexpected reluctance to leave. Part of that was because of Wilder, but she blamed the rest on nesting hormones. Pregnant women, she'd read, want to settle in during these last weeks and make a home for the baby.

If she left Mercy, her baby wouldn't have a home. But leaving was the deal she and Wilder had made when Wilder had agreed to let her stay on his ranch. As soon as she could travel, she'd give him back his house, take her baby and leave.

A deal was a deal. Even if it broke her heart.

Wilder roped a few dozen calves at Jess's place while Taylor was gone to her doctor's visit. He'd offered to go along, but she'd refused. Even though he had no right to be there, he'd wanted to go. In spite of knowing he shouldn't be bothered, the rejection had stung.

His brain understood her reasons, but convincing his heart was a challenge.

His greatest challenge, however, was defending her from Rob and Vivian Gadsden. He was working on that.

In fact, the time of practice on Jess's ranch had proved fruitful in more ways than one. His roping was hitting on all cylinders. He was tuned up and ready for next weekend's events in Wichita Falls. Sometimes his gut said he would win and this was one of those times.

Additionally, Jess had given him the name of a good lawyer. The attorney was outlandishly expensive, but, according to Jess, she was five feet two inches of effective powerhouse.

While waiting for Taylor to return home from the doctor, Wilder made a call to his banker, then cleaned the horse trailer and refreshed the linens in his camper. Since he didn't want Taylor mucking out the chicken pen, he did that too, along with some general cleanup and repair around the pens and barn.

He spent another hour working on the new horse facilities, mostly to work off nerves. He'd hoped to be finished and ready to fill the stalls and start training by next spring, but now he didn't know if that would be possible. Taylor and the baby had to come first, even if keeping them safe cost him his savings.

He was washing up under the water hose when Taylor's Toyota entered the yard. Shaking off the excess water, Wilder headed inside and toweled his face and arms in the kitchen.

The room smelled like lavender, a fragrance he'd always relate with Taylor, even after she left. Maybe he'd buy a candle or two to keep around the place. Or a box of her lavender goat soap.

She entered the kitchen, toting a grocery bag.

Wilder tossed the towel on the counter and took the bag.

"How'd it go?" he asked.

"Great. No problems, I guess."

Wilder frowned as he took out the orange juice and a head of something green. Weird lettuce, maybe. "What do you mean, *you guess*? What did the doc say?"

"Baby is on schedule in about two and half weeks."

"That's all?" Shouldn't there be more information by now?

She reached around him for the orange juice and took it to the fridge. "Pregnancy is old hat to an ob-gyn."

"Not to me." He corrected himself. "Or you."

She shrugged. "Flora's in love with that cat."

It took him a second to switch gears. "You were over there again."

"Since she dislikes going into town, I pick up groceries for her sometimes. She doesn't even have a phone, you know, so I have to stop in."

Wilder sighed. Arguing with this woman was useless. "Promise you'll be careful, okay?"

"I am." The grocery sack crinkled as she bumped him out of the way and emptied the remaining contents onto the counter. She held up a big package. "Want fried chicken for dinner? I'm in the mood to cook for somebody besides myself and the little guy."

"Are you kidding me? Homemade fried chicken? I could kiss you." He hadn't meant to blurt the last. Or maybe he had. Kissing her again sounded pretty good.

She turned toward him, her lips curving.

Oh, those beautiful, soft, bowed lips.

In spite of his hopeless situation, he leaned in for a brief, friendly smooch. Just a touch of his lips to hers. Though everything in him wanted to kiss her with all the love and passion in his heart, he kept himself on a tight rein.

The package in her hand thudded against the counter. A small, pleased hum escaped her. *Pleased.*

Someday, after she'd left—and he knew she would—he'd take out the memories of every kiss, every smile, every moment with Taylor and relive them over and over again.

When he eased back, bemused by the emotions dancing through him, Taylor patted his cheek the way she liked to do. "Don't be too thrilled. I've never fried chicken before."

"Want some help?"

Both her eyebrows lifted. "You know how?"

"No, but if we put our two heads together, I'm convinced we can do anything."

"I wish that was true."

"You're thinking about the Gadsdens' custody threat."

"I can't *stop* thinking about it."

"Me either. When I was at Jess's ranch earlier, I talked to him. I hope you don't mind, but if anyone had ideas, I knew Jess would."

"I don't mind. Jess has been nice to me."

"He's a good man. The best."

She clenched her hands in front of her belly. "What did he think?"

"We need an attorney." If she noticed his use of *we*, she didn't say anything. "He knows one who is every bit as good as Rob Gadsden. Maybe better."

Her hand went to her mouth. She gnawed at the fingernail. "I can't afford a lawyer right now, Wilder."

"I can. I called the bank. My savings should be enough."

Depending on the cost, a legal bill could wipe him out, but he'd cross that bridge when he came to it.

"No." She touched her fingertips to the middle of his chest. Could she feel his heart pounding? "I won't let you. That money is saved so you can start your horse training facility. The barn is almost finished. Using that money will set you back for years."

She was right, and he wished he'd never told her about his hope to settle down when this rodeo season ended with enough money to invest in his ranch. He'd almost attained that goal. A trip to the finals would secure the dream.

But Taylor and his nephew mattered more.

"Nothing says I can't keep rodeoing for a few more years." He didn't want to, but he could.

"You're number sixteen, all because of me. I won't let you lose another dream when you're this close."

"I'll regain my lead this weekend. Don't give it another thought." Let him do the worrying. "I'm talking about my money, and if I want to hire a lawyer for you, I will."

He had a stake in this thing too. She was expecting his nephew, the only relative he had any hope of building a relationship with—if Taylor would let him, and he thought she would.

"No use arguing, Wilder. I'll refuse to cooperate." She placed her hand on his cheek again. He loved when she did that. "I care too much about you to be the reason you throw away everything you've worked for."

Care. A gentle, friendly word that held such painful meaning to a man who wanted more than friendship.

"I care about you too," he said, the words gruff, "and that baby. You need my help and I'm going to give it."

The last words were a mistake. He saw the shift in her blue eyes. He'd hit a familiar nerve.

She stiffened. "This baby is my responsibility and mine alone. I can take care of myself. And him."

"Granted," he said, mostly to calm her. Nothing

she said would stop him now. He felt a powerful sense of responsibility for his nephew. And for Taylor. "But Scripture says two are better than one."

Her eyes narrowed. She perched a hand on one hip. "Oh, that was low. Using God to get your way."

"I'm doing this for you and baby, not me."

She dropped her head back and looked at the ceiling. "I know. I know. But I don't need your money."

"You don't?"

She sighed, shoulders lifting and falling. She pressed her lips together, sighed again and admitted, "If it comes down to hiring a lawyer, Wilder, I can get the money. I don't need your savings."

Wilder blinked, stunned. "You can get the money? How? Where? You're alone and barely keeping your head above water financially."

She shifted her gaze away from his and swallowed. "That's not exactly true. I never said I was alone. You assumed."

She seemed pretty alone to him. "But you *are* estranged from your family. Right? At least that's what you told me."

Taylor shook her head. "I never used the word *estranged*. I said my relationship with my family was complicated."

He parked a hand on each pocket of his jeans. A real bad feeling crept over him. "Maybe you should clear things up for me. This dumb cowboy can't seem to comprehend. Do you or do you not have a relationship with your family?"

"I do. Sort of." A furrow appeared in her forehead. "My family is wonderful. They love me, maybe too much. But they'll be there for me if I really need them. I just don't want to need them."

A deadly stillness came over him. "You lied to me?"

"Only by omission. If you knew I had family as close as the next town, would you have let me stay here?"

"In the *next town*? Are you serious?" Wilder squeezed a thumb and finger against his temples. He thought his head might blow up. She had family in the next town and didn't see them? Who did that? What was wrong with her? "I'd have told you to go home."

"Exactly. And I don't want to go home. So, technically, I didn't lie. I just didn't tell you everything."

A lie was a lie in his book. All this time she'd misled him. All this time he'd stressed about her being pregnant and alone, like his mom. He'd rushed home from each rodeo weekend to be with her, to make sure she was safe and well. He'd fallen in the standings because she needed him.

And all this time, she'd lived a lie.

Taylor watched the change come over Wilder. His expression, tender and concerned moments before, hardened.

"You're telling me that you have a loving family somewhere who would have willingly taken you in, and you're too proud to go to them?"

When he put it that way, she cringed, but refused to back down.

"I want to be my own person. Don't you get it? I need to succeed without their help. Or yours. Or anybody's."

Although in actuality, Wilder had been her refuge, her strength for months now. The difference being that he wasn't holding her back the way her granddad and sisters did.

"Let me explain—"

He karate-chopped the air with the side of his hand, effectively silencing her.

Oh, yeah. He was upset.

"You lied to me, Taylor. I'm having trouble with that. If I had a family who loved me, I wouldn't reject them. Certainly not for a ridiculous reason."

Taylor bristled. "My reasons are not ridiculous. My sisters and granddad smother me with their hovering. They want complete control of everything."

"Are you saying they mistreat you?"

"Of course not. They're good people. But they think I'm fragile and inept. If I go home, they'll take over my whole life again."

"You don't know that. Maybe they'll treat you like an adult about to have a baby, regardless of your foolishness."

Foolishness?

Taylor's back stiffened. Fire began to burn in her belly. "There is nothing foolish about wanting to be my own person."

Wilder's nostrils flared. His face darkened. With controlled fury in every word, he spat, "I'd give my left arm to have what you've rejected. Don't you understand how important family is?"

The man who never appeared riled was riled now. At her.

Well, she was riled too. This was her business, not his.

"Of course I do," she snapped. "But not like this." She swept a hand over her enlarged belly. "When I go home, it's on my terms, not because I'm desperate."

Wilder hissed through bared teeth.

"My entire life I've yearned for family. How could you possibly not want something so wonderful? How could you *lie* about them as if they were criminals?"

He didn't understand how hopeless she'd been when she'd left her family's ranch. No matter how much she explained, he was stuck on one technicality—a lie of omission.

"Obviously, you don't want to see my viewpoint." She jerked a skillet from the cabinet and slammed it onto the stove. "Fine."

"And you can't or won't see mine." With a wounded groan, he scrubbed both hands over his face. He was quiet for a moment and when he spoke, his voice had gone soft and sad. "Family is everything in this life, Taylor, the greatest earthly gift, and you have one that loves and wants you."

And he didn't.

What he said was true. Family *was* important, especially to a man who'd never had one.

Heat rose in her cheeks. "It's not like I've shut them out of my life completely. I talk to them on the phone."

With a bitter shake of his head, he said, "You let me believe the worst. That you were alone, abandoned, like me. How could you do that, Taylor?"

She heard the betrayal in his tone. And he was right. She'd let him believe she was without supportive family, the way he was.

"Did you even tell them about the baby?"

Taylor stared down at the skillet, stomach too sick to cook anything now.

Mouth dry with guilt, she muttered, "Not yet."

"Not yet?" His voice rose again. "They deserve to know, Taylor. You should be with them right now. Not here with a stranger, alone half the time."

"You're not a stranger." Not anymore.

"I didn't think so either, but now I'm not sure I know you at all."

She started toward him, apologies on her tongue, although she didn't know why she should. She'd done nothing wrong. Had she?

Before she reached him, Wilder sidestepped.

"I'll leave some money on the counter if you need anything for your trip. If I hurry, I can make a rodeo tonight."

He was leaving? But the Wichita Falls fair wasn't until next weekend.

The truth settled over her, heavy and painful.

There were other rodeos besides Wichita Falls, and though he hadn't planned to enter them, he would now. He was leaving because of her.

He couldn't stand the sight of her in his house anymore.

Sorrow clenched a fist in her chest. "Wilder, please. Let's talk about this."

He lifted both palms, then let them fall. "You don't belong here, Taylor. Go to your family. Where you and your baby should have been all this time. Not here with me."

Hot with emotion, and belly cramping, Taylor hugged her unborn baby and fought tears. "Don't leave like this. We can be friends, can't we?"

"Friends?" His gravelly voice throbbed with unspoken emotion. "I don't want to be friends anymore, Taylor."

The words were a sharp stab to her heart. "What about your nephew?"

"You know where to find me. If he needs me, wants me, I'll be here for him. Always."

Just not for her. Not anymore.

She heard what he didn't say. He wouldn't forsake his nephew the way his father had forsaken him, the way she'd forsaken her family in pursuit of her own happiness.

Wilder gave her one more sad look as if it was his heart breaking instead of hers. "I love him, Taylor. I thought we—"

He started to say something more, then shook his head, took his Stetson from the coat hook by the door and walked out.

Unlike before, he hadn't told her when he'd return, and she was almost certain he wouldn't come home after one rodeo the way he had for weeks.

Though her head jumbled with a dozen questions and thoughts, one thing stood out. The man she loved was gone and he wanted her to be gone too.

Chapter Seventeen

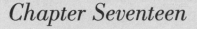

Long after Wilder's truck and trailer rig drove out of the yard, Taylor stood at the window staring down the road. She longed to call him or text him and beg him to return. Not that begging would do one bit of good. Wilder was a man of absolutes.

Inside him was the brokenhearted teenager rejected by his father, the only family he had left. He would never be able to understand why she avoided her sisters and granddad when they loved her and would welcome her with open arms.

She'd wounded him by shading the truth…

Bowing her head against the cool windowpane, she tried to pray. No answer. Nothing. No peace either.

Was God mad at her, like she'd been at Him for so long?

Were white lies a bad thing? Wilder certainly thought so.

Filled with turmoil, she finally left the window, aware that the cowboy was not coming back today. Maybe not tomorrow or the next day either. Not until he was sure she was gone.

After putting away the rest of the groceries, she went out to the back patio to sit and think. Exhaustion settled on her like a heavy blanket, worse today than usual, although every day lately had been tiring.

Veronica ambled up, bell jangling in the country quiet.

Taylor sighed. She'd miss this.

Burying her face in the goat's neck, Taylor let the despair settle over her.

A rank goat smell invaded her space.

When she raised her face to gulp in fresh air, Veronica tilted her comical face and bleated.

Feathers fluttered as Esther flew down from atop the air-conditioning unit and landed on the goat's back.

She'd miss this silly goat and Esther and the other chickens. The warmhearted people of Mercy too. She'd even miss her grumpy neighbor, Flora.

Most of all, she'd miss a big, rugged cowboy with a heart of gold. Would he forgive her if she asked?

Except she didn't want to ask. She groveled for no one. Wouldn't allow anyone else to run her life.

Except Wilder hadn't tried to be her boss. He'd simply been here for her.

"I love him," she said to Veronica. "Even if he doesn't feel the same, he loves my baby."

It was the one concept that gave her hope. He loved his nephew, wanted to be part of his life, and she would never, *could* never, keep this child away from him.

The anxiety about Cale's parents tried to push in. They wanted to take the baby from her and Wilder both. Although he seemed determined not to let that happen, what could Wilder do? Now that he knew she had family, he certainly wouldn't empty his savings to hire a lawyer.

The goat bleated at her, then resumed munching leaves from the hibiscus next to the patio. For once, Taylor didn't stop her.

Her family would help, somehow, if she asked. The asking was the hardest part.

She'd wanted to go home a big success. Now, if anything, she was a worse failure than ever.

But she had to go somewhere fast, before the baby arrived and Cale's parents found out and slapped her with the threatened custody suit.

Wilder had told her to go home.

Clearly, he didn't want her *here* anymore.

Taking out her cell phone, she pressed the icon of her granddad. Might as well get this over with.

When he answered, she said, "Poppy. Hi. It's me."

"How ya doin', little girl?"

Little girl. Poppy still saw her as a child.

"Great." Another white lie. "How is everything on the Matheson Ranch?"

"Right as summer rain. Where are you today? Off in the Amazon jungles or some such place?"

She tried to laugh at his joke. The sound came

out more pitiful than happy. "That's what I called about."

"The Amazon jungle?"

This time she did laugh. A little. "No, Poppy. I was thinking about maybe—"

The words stuck in the back of her throat. She couldn't crawl home now. The humiliation was too much.

"Maybe what, little one?"

"Oh, nothing important." *Liar, liar.*

A quiet hum of silence tensed the air before Poppy moved on. "Monroe's getting geared up to marry that nice feller of hers. You're coming home for the weddin', aren't you?"

"Have they set a date?"

"Aw, I don't remember, but I know it's pretty soon. You'll have to ask her. They're invitin' only a little group of friends and family for a ceremony up at that fancy mansion of Nathan's."

Her middle sister had fallen for the owner of a dude ranch. Although the mansion on the property had set empty for years, Monroe had sent her photos of the restoration. Persimmon Hill Guest Ranch was gorgeous. She wanted to see it, wanted to attend her sister's wedding, but not this way.

"I'm happy for her." With every fiber of her being, Taylor was thankful that no one had attended her wedding to Cale. They didn't even know about it. Just as they didn't know about the baby.

She needed to tell them. Her baby could be at stake.

"Poppy?"

"Yep?"

"I—"

Still, the words wouldn't come. Not yet. She needed more time to think and formulate all the excuses she'd need for not telling them sooner.

Later, or tomorrow, she'd call and tell them. By then she'd have a plan in place. Right this minute, she was running on emotion and fatigue. She wasn't thinking clearly.

"Oh, nothing. You doing okay? How are the knees? And Miss Bea?"

"Fine. But hold on a minute. Back your wagon up a tad. I hear something in your voice. What's wrong?"

Taylor swallowed hard. "Nothing."

"Darling, I raised you. I know when something's the matter. I know it in my knower. What is it?"

She drew her breath to spill everything, but finally settled on a half-truth. Another one. "Having a down day, that's all."

Tears gathered in her eyes. Her life was a wreck. She'd finally found the right man and now, she'd lost him. Him and everything else on this little ranch that had won her heart.

Poppy's voice nudged her. "Anything I can help with?"

"No." She kept the answer short, aware that

every word revealed too much of what she was feeling.

"Sure wish you'd come home. Whatever's troubling you, we can fix it. Me and your sisters. We'll take care of everything, like always. You're our baby girl."

Taylor cringed. That's what she was afraid of.

With tears about to choke her, she had to get off this call. "I love you, Poppy. Gotta run. Busy day."

Busy packing. Busy trying to figure out her next move.

"Love you too. I'm praying for you. Every day. You come on home when you're ready."

Considering the mess she'd made, would she ever be ready?

Taylor ended the call and the tears came in earnest.

Her stomach ached too much to eat, but she went inside for juice. As she passed through the living room, she spotted Wilder's big study Bible. Whenever he was home, they read and discussed a section together.

She'd learned more from him than she'd ever learned from Poppy, probably because she finally paid attention.

Setting her juice glass on a coaster, she opened the Bible and flipped through the pages, unsure of what she wanted to find, but searching nonetheless.

As if illuminated, a passage in Mark seemed to stand out.

Out of the heart of men, proceed evil thoughts, adulteries, fornications, murders, thefts, covetousness, wickedness, deceit, lasciviousness, an evil eye, blasphemy, pride, foolishness: All these evil things come from within, and defile the man.

She frowned at the page, trying to comprehend why this passage in particular had grabbed her attention. She wasn't a murderer! Or any of those awful things.

Wilder had called her foolish, but she disagreed.

Frowning, she read and reread, dissecting each word and eliminating herself as guilty until she came to the term *deceit.*

Had she been deceitful? Was a lie of omission the same as deceit?

Taking out her phone, she looked up the definition of deceit. The results stunned her.

She read aloud. "'Deliberate and misleading concealment, false declaration, or artifice.'"

Deliberate, misleading concealment. This was exactly what she'd done when Wilder had asked about her family. She'd misled him, concealed the truth.

Taylor leaned back against the chair cushion, stricken.

Although she'd considered her white lies to be inconsequential, she was guilty of deceit, something God considered evil. Like murder! Now, she understood why. Her lie, no matter how small, had caused grief for herself and wounded others. Like Wilder.

Poppy, Harlow and Monroe would also be hurt when they learned that she was about to have a baby, and all this time she'd been only a few miles away.

Wilder was right. Her behavior was foolish. Cruel. Dishonest.

She had to make this right.

Finding the cowboy's handsome face on her phone contacts, Taylor shot him a text. I'm not leaving here until we talk. I was wrong. I'm sorry.

She started to type I love you, but thought better of it, ending instead with a broken-heart emoji.

Holding the phone against her chest, she waited several long moments but no reply came.

Sooner or later, he'd have to come home.

A new stressor niggled the edges of her mind. Sometimes Wilder stayed gone for months, traveling the rodeo circuit. Right now, he needed every possible event if he wanted to make the National Finals.

She wanted his dream fulfilled. But she also wanted one more chance to ask forgiveness and make him realize how much he meant to her. Texts and calls were too easily misconstrued. Love demanded a face-to-face encounter. She needed to read Wilder's expression, to be held in his arms again, to feel his steadfast heart beat against hers.

If he rejected her apology—and her love—then and only then, she would leave for good.

Meanwhile, as Poppy would say, she had other fences to mend. Her family.

They'd be shocked, but, as Wilder suggested, they'd wrap loving arms around her and welcome her home.

The family ranch was less than twenty minutes away. Tomorrow, she'd go home to visit, then rush back here to wait for Wilder.

"Jesus, forgive me. Help me fix this. Somehow."

No matter how upset Wilder was, one fact remained. He'd promised to protect Taylor and the baby from his birth father's custody threat. And Wilder was a man who didn't break promises.

As he drove, he prayed and pondered. Taylor claimed her family would help her financially if needed. Was she too stubborn and proud to ask?

When push came to shove, he thought she was too smart not to. She loved that baby.

So did he. So he was taking no chances of the Gadsdens causing an issue for Taylor.

Wilder pressed two fingers to his sternum. His chest ached like heartburn that no number of TUMS would cure.

He could not get his nephew out of his mind, nor the threat his birth father had leveled at Taylor. Any man who rejected a woman who'd loved him and the son she bore him was cruel enough to follow through.

As Wilder drove and prayed, an idea came to mind that he could only credit to God. He certainly wasn't that smart.

Using the Bluetooth on his phone, he googled Rob Gadsden's law offices in Colorado and connected.

"Law offices of Gadsden and Fields. How may I direct your call?"

"Rob Gadsden, please." He slowed the truck and pulled to the side of the road.

"May I ask who's calling?"

"Wilder Littlefield. Tell him it's a family emergency."

"Please hold."

In seconds, an angry voice demanded, "What do you want? I've warned you not to bother me again with your ludicrous claims."

"Afraid I'll tell your secretary that I'm your son?"

"You are not my son."

The rejection still had the power to pierce through Wilder like a sharp sword.

Stiffening against the jab, he said, "DNA will prove that I am."

There was a pause on the other end, and Wilder knew he'd struck a nerve. "You'd need a court order for that."

"Actually, *Dad*, I wouldn't. I'm about to have a

nephew and his DNA will prove that I am his paternal uncle, which means I'm your son. Any court of law will agree."

Another pause before Rob began to sputter and spew. "Are you threatening me?"

"I don't make threats. I'll simply reveal the hard, scientific evidence that proves you're my father. I might even take out an ad in the Colorado Springs newspaper, proclaiming my delight in finding my birth father at last and realizing what a fine upstanding citizen he is. We could even end up on one of those reunion TV shows."

"You are a pathetic, worthless, gold-digging loser."

The insult turned Wilder's stomach. "I want no money from you."

"Then what do you want? Why do you insist on disrupting my family and causing anguish to my wife? She's required years to realize what a liar you are."

There was the crux. Rob did not want his wife to see the proof. She'd accepted his lies. DNA would take off the blinders.

Wilder hated what he had to do, but knew he must, not for himself, but for Taylor and the baby.

"You've threatened someone I love and I want you to stop. Two someones, actually—Taylor and my nephew."

"We have a right to that child."

"As a grandparent, maybe, but custody? No. Not

happening." Wilder spoke softly but with grit and gravel in his tone. "Taylor is a fine woman and she'll be a terrific mother. So, here's what I want from you, *Dad*."

Although dealing with Gadsden left a bad taste in his mouth, Wilder had promised to fight for Taylor's rights, no matter how she'd deceived him. This was his only ammunition. Lawyers cut deals all the time. He was fairly certain Gadsden was a master dealmaker.

"What deal? What are you talking about? And stop calling me Dad. What do you want that will make you go away forever?"

The last stabbed deeper. Wilder wondered if a heart could bleed from rejection.

Didn't matter. Not anymore. Only one thing did and that was to silence Rob Gadsden and his threats.

"I want a written, notarized statement that neither you nor anyone else will fight for custody of Taylor's child."

"You're delusional."

"Let me finish. In exchange for that written document, I will forget the DNA test that will prove you're my birth father."

Gadsden didn't answer. The line hummed while Wilder prayed and waited.

Finally, in a tone as crisp as if he was doing business with a criminal, Rob said, "I expect a similar document from you that you will drop your claim on me and renounce any claims of paternity on my part."

Wilder swallowed a lump of sorrow. The boy in him mourned. He'd always held out hope that someday Rob Gadsden would soften and claim him. If he made this agreement, all hope was gone.

If he didn't, Taylor would face a long, difficult battle with a cruel, selfish man.

Licking dry lips, he knew what he had to do. "Email me the paperwork and I'll sign it…after I receive yours."

As soon as he gave Rob his address, the man slammed the phone in his ear.

With his pulse pounding in his temples, Wilder sat in his truck on the side of the road for several more moments. He scrubbed both hands over his face, took a long drink of water from the thermos in his cupholder and then pulled back onto the highway.

He'd done the right thing for Taylor and now he had to tell her.

The phone seemed too impersonal. They'd left too much dangling between them. He couldn't just call her up and say, "Hey, your problem is solved. Bye."

He needed to talk to her face-to-face and hand her Rob's promised document in person.

Truth was—and he was a truth-teller even if Taylor wasn't—he wasn't ready to let go.

Would Taylor leave while he was gone? He had

mixed feelings, knowing she should go home to her family but reluctant to lose her.

She'd wronged him, but he was commanded to forgive her.

How would he concentrate on tonight's event when all he could think about was Taylor, her deception, her family, the baby he wanted for his own and the major mess he'd left behind?

He'd never planned on falling in love, but love had a way of sneaking up on a man when he wasn't looking. Or in his case, moving into his house while he wasn't home.

As he reached the rodeo arena and parked his trailer alongside two dozen others, he tried to refocus. Tonight, he needed a win. Tomorrow, his head would be clearer and he could figure out what to do about Taylor and her son.

Taylor packed an overnight bag. She couldn't move back in with her family today. Not until she'd made arrangements for her animals. However, she could drive to the Matheson Ranch for a surprise visit. *Surprise* being the operative word. When she walked through the front door and they saw her pregnant body, how would they react?

She was nervous about finding out. But she had to go. Not only because Wilder insisted, but because he was right and she was wrong.

What she really wanted was a long nap. She was

unusually tired, though she figured the cause was emotional turmoil and late-term pregnancy.

Her back ached something terrible and as she bent over the dresser drawer for clean pajamas, her head spun. She grabbed the dresser top and straightened. A sharp pain sliced across her middle.

She gasped, held her breath and waited for the pain to subside. Her vision blurred.

Holding to the wall, she stumbled to the bathroom to be sick.

What in the world?

The dizziness came again, worse this time. She held to the bathroom sink. Unable to remain upright, she slid to the floor.

The sharp pain in her right abdomen stole her breath. She panted, fighting another wave of nausea.

For several long, miserable moments, she leaned her head against the bathroom wall and took deep, slow breaths.

Finally, the strange sensations subsided.

Though wobbly, she rose and finished packing a bag. Wilder was right—she was a foolish woman. She'd never been afraid before. Now, she was afraid for herself and for her child.

If anything went wrong with the pregnancy, she was alone and miles from the nearest hospital. The decision was no longer hers to make. She had to go home.

Having already secured and tended the animals, she gathered her belongings, grabbed her cell phone, locked Wilder's house and started the twenty-mile drive to her hometown in the valley.

As she reached the curve and neared Flora's house, pain stabbed behind her eyes. Her head throbbed and the dizziness returned.

Was she about to pass out?

Taking no chances on having an accident, she eased off the gas and guided the car into Flora's driveway.

The front door of the house opened. Flora stepped out, a hand shading her eyes.

Taylor stumbled from the car, knees wobbling.

"I'm sick." She weaved, flung both arms out to regain her balance. "Help."

Just when she thought she'd go down, a surprisingly strong Flora shoved a shoulder beneath her armpit and led her inside the house.

Exhausted, Taylor tumbled into a recliner.

Flora stood over her, glaring. "What's wrong? Is the baby coming?"

"No. I don't know. No." Breath short and rapid, Taylor grasped her head. "My head. I'm dizzy. Sick."

Flora touched two fingers to her wrist while the other hand felt the top of Taylor's belly before pressing an ear against the same spot.

"Give me your phone." The woman tugged at Taylor's fingers.

Realizing she still clutched the device in one hand, Taylor released it. Flora hurried out of the room.

Taylor couldn't think straight enough to worry that Flora might not return or that if she did, she'd do something sinister.

When an old-fashioned, manual blood pressure cuff wrapped around her upper arm, Taylor opened aching eyes to meet the woman's sharply intelligent stare.

"You're a midwife?" she whispered through trembling lips.

Flora grunted. "Not anymore. We've got to get you out of here before they find out."

Find out what? Who were they? The words formed on Taylor's tongue, but she never knew if she spoke them or not.

Flora released the air and pumped the cuff again. She hissed out a worried breath.

Grumbling, tone tense and gruff, the former midwife checked vital signs and then pressed a stethoscope against Taylor's belly.

After a minute of listening, she barked out, "I told you to keep an eye on that blood pressure. What's wrong with you, girl? Have you no sense? Where's that cowboy of yours?"

"Gone."

"Figures. Pretends to care but who knows his motives?"

That wasn't Wilder at all.

"Not his fault."

Flora harrumphed. "You need magnesium sulfate and you need it fast. In a hospital."

Storming around the sparse living room, she muttered aloud, though Taylor missed most of the words. She couldn't seem to stay awake. The pain in her head grew worse.

"I've called 9-1-1. They're too far away. By the time they get here, it may be too late."

Taylor heard the last all too clearly. Too late for what?

She did not want to know. Struggling, she sat up. "Take me."

"You don't know what you're asking, girl. I won't go back. I can't have anything happen in my house either." She dropped her head back and groaned. "What was the man thinking to leave you this close to delivery?"

"My fault."

Flora stared down for three beats, a dozen emotions moving across her wrinkled face as she struggled with what to do.

At last, she pressed her thin lips together and gave one hard nod as if she'd made up her mind. "Can you walk to the car?"

"I'll try." She had to. *God help me. God help my baby.*

Using her last bit of energy, she pushed out of the chair, blood pressure cuff dangling from her arm. She reached to remove it.

Flora interrupted her. "Leave it."

Again, the tone was gruff and angry but Flora grasped Taylor's arm, flung it over one shoulder and half carried, half walked her to the car.

For a skinny old woman, she was strong.

"Front seat," Flora said. "I want my eyes on you."

Could Flora drive? Taylor had never seen a car on the property besides her own.

Too sick and weak to ask, she fell into the passenger seat as soon as Flora opened the door.

The frail-looking woman was around the car and in the driver's seat faster than seemed possible for a woman her age. In seconds, they were on the road, speeding toward Centerville.

"What's wrong with me?" Taylor whispered.

"I'm not a doctor," she snapped. "Don't ask."

But Flora knew. Taylor could hear in her voice that the former midwife recognized her condition and wasn't talking, which meant the answer was bad.

A chill ran through Taylor. She shivered.

Hands cradling her unborn infant, she turned a frightened gaze on her rescuer. "Don't let my baby die."

"Shut up." Flora's furious glare silenced her.

Neither said another word all the way to Centerville Hospital.

Taylor had never been so scared in her life. She thought Flora might feel the same.

They were in trouble. Real trouble.

Chapter Eighteen

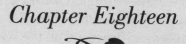

"You're up next, Wilder."

A half dozen cowboy bodies leaned on the back stalls to watch the action out in the arena. The spectacle of an all-American PRCA Rodeo was under way, complete with TV cameras and a large, appreciative crowd in the stands.

Wilder ran his hands down Huck's cannon and fetlock, adjusting the protective boots for best support. With a final tug on the saddle girth, he stuck his piggin' string between his teeth and mounted the dependable roping horse.

He'd drawn a good calf the last go-round and posted a big score. Two more good scores would go a long way toward moving him up where he needed to be.

The current calf, already in the stall, would give him a run for it, but he'd seen this steer before and thought he and Huck could beat him.

Huck was quick as a flea hop and steadier than a mountain. As long as the roper did his job, Huck would handle the rest.

Wilder backed his horse into the box, adjusted the piggin' string and readied his rope.

Adrenaline began to build in his veins. Around

him conversations mingled with clanking metal and the calls of livestock. The PA system announced his name, bragging on the fine horse and commenting on Wilder's first real push toward the finals.

He tried to drown any thoughts except the task before him.

The argument with Taylor pushed in. If only she'd been completely forthcoming about her situation—

During that split second of distraction, the calf broke free into the arena. Huck jerked as if to ask why Wilder wasn't urging him on.

Adrenaline stinging his veins, Wilder gave Huck his head. The dependable horse shot after the calf, though they were far behind.

Wilder swung the rope wide and long, made the catch, already sliding from the saddle as Huck jabbed his hooves into the dirt and skidded to a stop.

One hand sliding down the rope, Wilder raced to the calf and quickly made the tie. He tossed his hands into the air, stopping the time clock. Frustrated, he walked back to his horse and mounted to wait the required seconds to be sure the calf stayed tied. Wilder knew before his time blared over the PA that they'd been slow.

His fault. Too distracted.

The calf was released, and he and Huck moseyed out of the arena to tepid applause. As they made their way down the alley behind the chutes, other horse and rider teams meandering about, heaviness rested on Wilder's chest.

He'd placed first in the opening event. Unless the remaining cowboys did worse, this round he'd likely be out of the money. One more chance tomorrow night before he moved on to Wichita Falls.

As he unsaddled Huck and rubbed him down, Taylor returned to his thoughts. He hoped she was doing okay. In spite of his disappointment, he worried about her and the baby.

He didn't like the way they'd left things.

Should he send a text to check on her and tell her not to stress about Rob Gadsden because he had good news? Stress was bad for her and the baby.

After tying Huck behind the trailer to graze, he'd retrieved his cell phone from the truck cab and started back to the arena to watch the rest of the rodeo when his ringtone sounded.

Pausing in the shade and relative quiet of another cowboy's rig, he opened the device and noticed a text he hadn't seen before. From Taylor.

His heart jumped.

He answered the phone call first.

"Who? Yes, this is Wilder Littlefield. What's going on?" As he listened, every muscle in his body tensed. His pulse began to thrum louder and louder. "Where? Is she…?"

Fear spurting through him like a geyser, Wilder spun and ran for the truck. "I'm on my way."

* * *

Wilder's boot heels clicked with rapid insistence against the spotless white tile as he hurried down the long, wide corridors of Centerville Hospital. The disinfectant and antiseptic scents were familiar. Most rodeo cowboys spent some time in emergency rooms or in visiting other cowboys, but today someone far more important to him had been admitted.

The front desk had given him a room number but refused to give out further information. He wasn't family. Accustomed as he was to those kinds of comments, today he felt their sting more than usual.

The baby he'd begun to think of as his own, or at least whom he loved as much as he thought a father would, was somewhere in this place.

Had he arrived yet? Was he okay? Was Taylor? Flora's call had been terse and quick, leaving him with more questions than answers. All she said was that Taylor and the baby were in danger and on the way to the hospital.

Sweat dampened Wilder's palms. Every ounce of resentment he'd felt about Taylor's lies drained out of him, one worried drop of sweat after another.

He loved her. Her health and his nephew were what mattered now, not his tender feelings. She'd had her reasons and he'd refused to listen, riding his self-righteous high horse out the door.

Let him without sin cast the first stone.

The quote wasn't exact, but the idea was right on target.

"Yeah," he muttered as he reached the door bearing the room number he'd been given. The heavy wooden structure was closed tight. Inside he heard voices.

Heart in his throat, he tapped lightly with a knuckle.

A gorgeous blonde with hair covering one side of her face opened the door. She stared at him, none too friendly. "Yes?"

Wilder removed his hat. "Is Taylor in this room?"

The blonde raked him with a cold glare. "Who are you?"

"Name's Wilder. Is Taylor okay?"

"Monroe, let him in."

Wilder recognized that voice. Taylor was inside and able to speak.

Heart pounding, he inwardly gave thanks. "Please, I have to see her."

With an insolent huff, the blonde opened the door wider. He edged past her, eager to see for himself that the woman he loved was safe and well.

A herd of people crowded the room like too many calves in a chute, but he ignored them and zeroed in on the patient. Taylor lay in a mountain of white sheets, hooked to beeping monitors, wires and dangling tubes.

In her arms was a blanket-wrapped bundle.

Every cell in Wilder's body yearned toward both of them.

He crossed the space, longing to touch her but holding tight to his hat.

Taylor's eyes searched his. He saw the caution in them, but also the hope. Was she glad he was here?

"How did you know? What are you doing here?"

"Flora called me." He shifted and heard his boots scrape the tile. Had he cleaned his boots after the rodeo? He didn't think so. He'd been in too much of a hurry. "Scared five years off my life."

"She saved mine. Mine and Stetson's." Taylor dipped her head tenderly toward the blue bundle.

"Stetson? I like that. Good cowboy name." Still gripping the hat that shared a name with Taylor's son, Wilder wished for things he couldn't have. He'd come to right a wrong, not cause more problems. The ball was in her court.

"I thought so too. Stetson reminds me of you. You always wear that hat." Her smile was sweetly teasing as she glanced from him to the tiny blue bundle. "Do you want to hold him?"

She'd named her baby as a reminder of him? What could that mean?

Hope, like a fragile butterfly, fluttered in.

"Can I? Is it okay? Is he all right? I don't want to hurt him. Flora said—"

A wiry old man with white hair who must be her grandfather spoke up. "They were touch and go for a spell. Gave us all a scare. But docs say they're doing good now."

Wilder's eyelids fell shut. "Thank God."

"Yes, sir. We sure do." The man stuck out a hand. "Wilder, I'm Gus Matheson, Taylor's granddad. She told us about you."

"She did?" Wilder turned back to Taylor. She confirmed with a nod and a tired lift of bow lips.

With his heart on fire, he longed to tell her how much she and Stetson meant to him. To let her know how empty his life was without her and how he'd been so afraid of losing her after Flora's phone call.

But not in a crowd of people. He wanted to know her reaction first before he made a fool of himself in front of the world.

"Sure did," Gus said. "She kept asking for you, wanting you here to take charge of Stetson if something should happen to her."

The shock of the older man's words jerked his head up. "You'd want me to take Stetson? Me?"

"Yes. You." She stirred to rearrange the baby in her arms. "Now, are you going to hold your nephew or stand there with your hat in your hand?"

"A Stetson in my arms sounds better than one in my hands."

Someone behind him—the blonde, he thought—slid his hat from his fingers. "Go wash your hands."

Gus chuckled. "Monroe's kinda bossy sometimes."

A bossy sister was one of the reasons Taylor stayed away from her family. From the look of things, she'd resolved that issue today. At least, he hoped she had. He sure was glad to see them gathered around her. Family was everything.

Wilder hustled over to the sink next to the door and scrubbed every germ from his hands and lower arms.

He didn't think he'd ever been quite this excited, not even when he'd won the all-around purse at a major rodeo.

As he extended his arms to take the baby, Taylor said, "Poppy, do you all mind waiting outside for a while? I need to talk to Wilder."

The old man smoothed his mustache and grinned. "Figured."

"We're hungry anyway," Monroe droned, one hip lower than the other. "You made us miss lunch."

A nice-looking guy with blue eyes draped an arm over Monroe's shoulders and said something about feeding her shrimp. She playfully elbowed his ribs and muttered, "Bottom feeders."

The group chuckled and jostled as they exited the room and closed the door behind them.

Wilder was pretty sure he heard the old man say, "Taylor's got herself a cowboy in love."

He wasn't wrong.

Looking into his nephew's squinched face, Wilder's insides erupted in a volcano filled with love. Every innate protective instinct known to man stirred in him. In that moment, Wilder knew he'd fight a grizzly bear bare-handed for this boy and his mother.

So this was love, he thought in amazement.

It was scary wonderful.

"He's perfect." Wilder met Taylor's eyes, saw his own awe reflected there. "Isn't he?"

"Five and a half pounds of perfection."

"I never knew—" he started and then stopped before he went too far. They had to talk before he spilled this wild emotion all over the place.

Aw, but he could not get over the feeling of this precious boy lying in his arms, warm, soft and completely innocent. Stetson was a blank slate at the mercy of adults to provide well and to guide his life in the right direction.

Lord, I have to be here for him. I love him. He needs me.

With a ferocity that surprised him, Wilder vowed to give this boy everything he himself had never had. Not just materially but emotionally and spiritually. This boy needed a man in his life and Wilder wanted to be that man.

If Taylor would agree. Whatever he had to say or do, he'd do it. He could not let them go.

Trembling inside with emotion, Wilder backed onto the chair someone had pushed behind his knees on their way out and sat, careful not to jostle the tiny infant.

So many questions swirled in his head. So much love and need he thought his chest would explode.

He sorted through his thoughts and found his way back to the beginning. "What happened? Was there an accident? Did you get hurt? You said Flora brought you. Where is she?"

Taylor lifted a tubing-covered hand from the sheets as if to slow him down. "Hospitals make her nervous after what she went through. She took my car home as soon as she knew Stetson and I would recover."

"So the rumors were true?"

"Yes, it's so sad, Wilder. She went to prison after a woman died giving birth. Even though Flora did nothing wrong, courts convicted her because her midwife license didn't cover the state where the birth took place. After two awful years in prison, she moved as far away from the gossip as possible and vowed never to let anyone close enough to accuse her of anything again. She lost all trust in people and in God."

"I'm sorry." He owed Flora lot more than a mowed lawn.

"Me too. She's a good person. As scared as Flora was that something bad would happen to me or Stetson and she'd be blamed and sent back to prison, she took care of me and drove me here. She didn't leave until she'd barked a dozen orders and made sure I was in good hands."

"I didn't even know she could drive." The baby in his arms mewed. Both adults paused to watch with rapt attention the tiny miracle of life stretch and snuggle.

When he'd settled again, never opening his wrinkled eyes, Wilder exchanged tender smiles with Taylor. "What happened? What was the emergency? Why all these scary wires and machines?"

"My blood pressure went haywire and I was in danger of going into seizures and losing Stetson. Preeclampsia."

"I don't even know what that is." But it sounded bad. "Are you still in danger?"

"I don't understand much about preeclampsia either. I was dizzy and sick and thought my head would explode. They said I could have had a stroke." She lifted her thin shoulders. "It's some kind of chemical imbalance I think."

Seizures or a stroke? The words struck fear in Wilder's soul. "Will it go away?"

"Docs say the worst has passed, but they're keeping us both for a few days to monitor my blood pressure and be sure." She peeled the blanket away from Stetson's tiny face, a softness about her that Wilder had never seen before. "He was distressed but recovered fast once they did the C-section and he could breathe on his own."

"C-section." This kept getting worse. He should have been here. Not that he could have done anything other than hold her hand and pray, but prayer was a big something. "Are you in pain?"

She motioned toward one of the IV bags bearing

several colorful stickers. "Not yet. Along with the magnesium they pumped me full of pain meds. I'm real happy right now. Especially with you here."

Wilder smiled, though nothing about her close call was funny. Thank God for Flora. He didn't even want to think about what would have happened if their neighbor hadn't been brave enough to take charge.

He never wanted anything like that to happen again.

"I got your text," he said. "You're right. I was wrong to leave that way. We need to talk things out. I owe you an apology."

"Not true. I deceived you, Wilder, and that's wrong. I read it in your Bible this morning. I'm the one who needs to apologize. I asked God to forgive me, and I promise never to shade the truth again, but I need your forgiveness too."

"Done."

She squeezed the forearm he'd wrapped around her baby. "That's what I love about you, Wilder Littlefield. You have the biggest heart in the world."

"Is that all you love about me? 'Cause I'm already crazy about this little cowboy of yours."

And you.

Wilder was about to stick his neck out. He knew he was, but he couldn't let her go without clearing the air between them.

She and Stetson were worth chancing another rejection.

* * *

Taylor had never been so glad to see anyone in her life than Wilder when he'd walked through the door. He'd looked harried and frightened and cowboy determined.

Even after she'd deceived and disappointed him, he'd rushed to her side as soon as Flora had made contact. Like her family had.

Though shocked, not one family member had blasted her the way she'd deserved. Like Wilder, they'd rallied around with love and a promise to look after her and Stetson.

This time she hadn't minded so much. If Flora hadn't been there to intervene, she and Stetson could have died.

She understood now. People need people. All this time she'd needed Wilder and he'd been right there for her, even though she had been too stubborn to realize it.

Now, with her family outside and this big cowboy offering the forgiveness she craved but didn't deserve, the room seemed lighter and happier.

"If your arms are getting tired, put him in the isolette."

"I like holding him, but he needs to rest. I read that in one of those baby care books you bought. Birth is tough for him too. He's tired."

Her heart melted. "You read one of my baby books?"

His look was sheepish. "I'm his uncle. I didn't want to mess up."

If that wasn't the sweetest thing, she didn't know what was. Wilder did sweet things all the time, and she'd been too self-focused to appreciate him.

Wondering how to tell him, she watched as he placed Stetson in the plexiglass crib. As carefully as if the baby was a burstable soap bubble, he tucked the blanket around him and, bending low, kissed the tiny baby's forehead.

Taylor's chest heated with love. Wilder and Stetson together looked right and good.

If only she and Wilder were a couple and this was their child…

For someone who'd wanted to travel—suddenly, settling down with the right man, *this man*, sounded wonderful.

Could he ever want her after all her mistakes? Did she dare ask?

Treading softly, while she inwardly navigated this new realization, she asked, "You're missing your rodeo, aren't you?"

Regaining the chair and tugging it close to the bed, Wilder brushed off the question. "There'll be other rodeos."

True, but when a rider's placement hung by a thread he needed every win.

"Thank you."

He titled his head. "For?"

"You've done everything for me, and all I've been is a burden to you."

"Not true." He folded his muscled forearm on her mattress and leaned in close. "In these past few months you've given me something I haven't had since Mom died."

His nearness set Taylor's heart into a rapid rhythm. The scent of his woodsy cologne circled her head. Oh, yeah, she loved this man. "What?"

"Someone to come home to." He swallowed and raised gentle brown eyes to hers. "Almost felt like a family."

A piece of her heart chipped off. This kind-hearted cowboy longed for family, something he hadn't had since he was sixteen.

She placed her palm against his cheek and he leaned into it. "I was feeling that way too."

His warms lips grazed her palm.

"Really? How are you feeling now?"

"Settled. I want a permanent home for me and my son."

"What about your travel blog?"

"I haven't worked everything out in my head yet, but the blog has evolved. With extra effort, I can turn it into a Mom blog or a craft vlog or some such."

"Staying in one place hasn't been your thing. Wouldn't you be restless to move on to the next adventure?"

She smiled at her son. "This is my greatest ad-

venture right here. Maybe I'll travel again some-day. Right now, the important thing is my son."
And you.

Drawing a breath, she hinted at what she really desired. "The past few months on the Three Nails Ranch have been the most content I've ever felt. The happiest. With you."

Wilder's rugged face grew serious as he pro-cessed her words. That was his way, she'd learned. Think before speaking. Process and understand. She hoped he understood what she was afraid to admit.

"Are you saying you want to come home to the ranch when the docs kick you out?"

"How would you feel about that?" She pressed her lips together, waiting, hoping.

"A more permanent arrangement sounds real good. If that's what you want. Stetson needs a man in his life who loves him."

"Is he the only reason?"

"Only you can answer that."

Taylor saw the caution in his eyes, aware of how many times in his life he'd been rejected. She never, ever wanted him to feel that way again. Not from her or Stetson.

"If you're asking if I want to continue our liv-ing arrangements the way they are," she said, "the answer is no."

His expression fell. He started to withdraw, but she grabbed his hand. "Wilder, listen to me. I'm a woman with a lot of baggage. I've made terrible mistakes. I lied to you. I don't know why you'd want me in your life at all, but I want to be there."

"When I was praying my guts out on the drive here, I was reminded that none of us is without sin. We all foul up, Taylor. That doesn't make you a bad person. It makes you a person who needs Jesus and the forgiveness only He can give." He shook his head. "Sorry. Didn't mean to preach."

"You didn't. Oh, Wilder, you are the best man I've ever known besides my Poppy. I don't deserve you, but I want you, not as a landlord who owns the house I've invaded and not only as a friend."

He stroked her cheek with the back of his fingers. "I want you too, Taylor, not as a housekeeper, although you do make a mighty fine lasagna, and not only as a friend who does interesting experiments in my kitchen." His expression softened until Taylor felt herself melting under the tenderness. "I'm in love with you, Taylor Matheson. So, I need to know. Do you love me?"

"How can you love me? I'm such a mess."

He shook his head, smile tender. "Answer the question, please. I'm not leaving until you do. Be honest. I'm a big boy and I can take it. If we're done, I'll walk away, no harm, no foul, but with lots of good memories."

More of the reasons she loved him so much.

Needing to touch him, to connect as only touch can, she placed her hand against his stalwart heart.

"I think I fell in love with you the very first night we met, even though I didn't know it then. I mean, what man gives up his entire house to a stranger?"

"Had no choice. You looked fierce wielding my black iron skillet. But real cute too."

They smiled into each other's face, reliving the memory together.

With love floating over them like a warmed blanket, Wilder was the first to speak. "Can we make this official, then? I love you, Taylor. If you and Stetson will have this old cowboy, I'm all yours. But the deal is forever. You as my wife. Stetson as my son."

"We will." Emotion big enough to choke an elephant welled up in Taylor's throat. "If you'll have us."

"I've wanted you both way longer than you know." Wilder leaned in to brush the hair back from her face.

She loved when he did that. His rough, rugged hand was as light and gentle as a feather.

Loving him more than she thought possible, Taylor kept her hand on his chest, felt his heartbeat and the rise and fall of his breathing. "I thought you were a confirmed bachelor. What happened?"

"You. Stetson. The two of you convinced me that I could love like a real man should, not selfishly like my father or brother. I always wanted family. I just didn't want to hurt anyone the way my father hurt my mother and me."

"Now, you listen to me, Wilder Littlefield. You *are* a real man. I saw it from the beginning when you gave up your home for a perfect stranger. You are nothing like Rob or Cale. Couldn't be if you tried. Stop worrying about suddenly becoming someone you could never be. You may share their DNA but your heart is all yours." She grabbed the neck of his T-shirt and gave a tug, refusing to care that any movement hurt her incision. "Got it?"

A smile bloomed across his rugged features.

"Got it. That means a lot to me. You and Stetson mean *everything* to me and I'll do all in my power to be the man you both need."

"I know that. You already have been."

"So, you'll marry me?"

"I will."

With a rueful twist of his mouth, Wilder motioned to the tubes and beeping machines. "This wasn't the most romantic place for a proposal. Sorry."

Taylor's shoulders lifted in a shrug that disturbed a mile of tubing. "Nothing about our relationship has been the norm, but I sort of like it that way. We're unique."

"Yeah." Wilder rubbed a hand over the back of his neck. "I guess we are. But I promise to take you someplace romantic the first chance we get and repropose."

She snickered. "Repropose? Is that a thing?"

His lips curved. "Well, I've proposed twice already so yeah, I guess it is. And I'm a man who keeps his promises."

She grabbed his collar again and pulled him down.

She kissed him, slow and sweet, as all the love she'd felt for weeks came to a crescendo.

When he straightened to his full height, expression pleased and bemused, he held up one finger. "Don't kiss me again. I'm losing my mind. Or at least my train of thought."

She laughed. "Is that a bad thing?"

"At the moment, yes. In all this excitement, I almost forgot. I have good news."

Wilder gingerly scooped the baby up again and cradled him against his broad chest. The sweet sight was enough to make Taylor teary, although she blamed hormones too.

"What kind of good news? This proposal of yours was pretty awesome. I can't imagine better."

"This little man," he said with fierce protectiveness, "is no longer in danger of a custody battle."

Taylor jerked upright in the bed. Her incision complained. "Really? How is that possible? How do you know?"

"I talked to Rob Gadsden. We made a deal of sorts and he agreed to a written statement disclaiming any right to Stetson, now and in the future."

Oh, Wilder, what have you done?

"How did you get him to agree to something like that? What kind of deal did you make?"

"A deal that cost me nothing that I hadn't already given him. Now, stop talking and say you love me again. I like the way it sounds."

"You're not my boss, Mister Cowboy, but I do love you. This time I know what real love is and it looks like you. Put our baby down so I can kiss you again and try to blow your mind."

"Too late. You already have."

As carefully as before and far too slowly for Taylor, Wilder eased Stetson back into his bed. After tucking the blankets snugly around the baby, he turned back to Taylor.

She gripped his stubbled jaw and kissed him with all the love inside her. To her great delight, Wilder kissed her back in the same way. Passion laced with joy and a love too big to keep to himself.

When the kiss finally ended, long after her heart had left her body and joined with his, he pressed his forehead against hers and said, "Wow. When are we getting married?"

She laughed. "ASAP, cowboy. ASAP."

Epilogue

The giant rodeo-inspired sheet cake, baked and decorated by none other than Miss Bea and Sage Trudeau of the Bea Sweet Bakery, said it all.

Stetson Gabriel Littlefield.

That's all. Just three words in baby blue icing that changed three lives forever. Stetson was officially, legally and forever the son of Wilder and Taylor Littlefield. And Wilder had the court papers to prove it.

He was a dad and a husband. He had a family.

Even now, he could hardly wrap his head around the last four months.

Heart and home full to overflowing with people he cared deeply about, Wilder moved among the gathered crowd getting better acquainted with Taylor's friends and family and welcoming his own friends. Jess was here, Pate and a few other cowboys and their families, along with Milly and Walt and other neighbors from the town of Mercy.

He'd quickly bonded with Taylor's family, especially her Poppy, Gus, an old cowboy with more sayings than Bartlett's book of quotations. Her sisters were all right too. Red-haired Harlow and blonde Monroe who hid facial scars behind her hair had married two really nice guys he liked as well. One was a pro football player with nary an arrogant bone in his body who was currently overseeing the brisket smoker in the backyard.

Surrounding the smoker were the Mathesons' close friends, the Trudeaus—a trio of jovial ranchers and their wives, including the stunningly beautiful baker, Sage.

A passel of kids ran through Wilder's small house playing space invaders. He still couldn't keep them all straight but clearly the Trudeaus were eager to have more. Bowie's wife, Sage, and Yates's wife, Laurel, were both expecting. Wade and Kyra seemed content with their triplets for the moment.

To his and Taylor's amazement, Flora had agreed to attend the celebration, and even now sat in a rocker crooning to Stetson while a half dozen other women gathered around her and Taylor to discuss all things baby and child-rearing.

She was beautiful, his new wife, glowing with happiness.

Every morning, he awoke awash in gratitude at how his life had changed in such a short time. He hadn't known how lonely he was until Taylor had invaded his home.

She glanced up from a conversation with Harlow and caught him staring.

Leaving the group, she wove her way to him. "Hey, cowboy. Want to marry me again?"

"Sure do. You available for the rest of your life?"

He looped an arm over her shoulders and snugged her close. "You smell good."

"Eau de Baby and goat soap."

"Love it. Love you. Love our son. I'm even getting attached to that goat of yours."

Grinning, she snaked an arm around his waist and cocked her head up at him. "No regrets about missing the rodeo finals?"

"I want to spend our first Christmas with you and Stetson, so no, none. What about you? Any regrets about settling in one boring spot with a failing cowboy?"

"Nothing boring about you. And you didn't fail. You postponed because of me. Besides, we'll do our share of rodeo traveling next season."

They would. He'd enter enough rodeos to complete his horse ranch, but he would take his wife and baby along with him. Taylor wanted to blog about the rodeo and ranching life. Already was. And to her surprise, her craft business was fast overtaking her success as a travel blogger. He'd known she'd be successful, and his chest swelled with pride at his incredible, entrepreneurial wife.

He couldn't predict tomorrow and wouldn't try. His dream of the National Finals might or might not be gone. Whatever God sent his way, Wilder rested in knowing it would be for his good.

He'd be content with the one blessing he'd never had but always desired. A family with the woman he loved and the sweet bonus of a little boy who not only shared his DNA and last two names, but who would, after today, forever call him Daddy.

This was the best dream of all...and he was living it.

* * * * *

Don't miss the previous books from
New York Times *bestselling author*
Linda Goodnight:

To Protect His Children
Keeping Them Safe
The Cowboy's Journey Home
Her Secret Son
The Rancher's Sanctuary

All are available now wherever
Love Inspired books are sold!